ALSO BY C

Jamison Valley Series

The Coppersmith Farmhouse

The Clover Chapel

The Lucky Heart

The Outpost

The Bitterroot Inn

The Candle Palace

Maysen Jar Series

The Birthday List

Letters to Molly

Lark Cove Series

Tattered

Timid

Tragic

Tinsel

Tin Gypsy Series

Gypsy King

Riven Knight

Stone Princess

Noble Prince

Runaway Series

Runaway Road

Wild Highway

Quarter Miles

Forsaken Trail

Dotted Lines

Standalones

Rifts and Refrains

PROLOGUE

"Are you sure about this?" Aria asked. She'd buckled her seat belt but hadn't closed the passenger door.

The ocean breeze drifted inside the cab and caught the flyaway hairs by my temple. One strand tickled my nose and another stuck to the gloss on my lips.

Was I sure about this?

No.

I wasn't sure about anything anymore. But that's what happened in life. You endured the moments of excruciating pain. A death. A heartbreak. A betrayal. You made decisions that would alter the course of your life in the hopes that there was something good waiting for you at the end of the road. You survived today to get to tomorrow.

Yesterday, I'd had a home. I'd had a job. I'd had a family.

Yesterday, I'd been in love.

1

But a lot had changed since yesterday. Even more had changed in the past five days.

My only wish was that tomorrow, some of this crippling heartache might fade. That the urge to scream and cry would wane.

There was only one way to find out.

I jammed the key into the ignition. "Close the door."

CHAPTER ONE

KATHERINE

F*ive days earlier...*
   Eight hundred and thirty-one miles.

My heart thumped harder as I stared at the number on the map. My breath caught in my throat. It was only a road trip but my stomach was in knots.

I hadn't left Montana since the day I'd arrived. As a fresh-faced and eager eighteen-year-old, I'd found safety here. A home. I'd rarely left the Greer Ranch and Mountain Resort, let alone the state, but I had to get out of here.

I needed every one of those eight hundred and thirty-one miles.

Excitement mixed with anxiety as I closed the GPS app on my phone with trembling fingers. Scanning my office, I racked my brain for anything I'd forgotten to do in my whirlwind attempt to prepare for this no-notice, yet overdue vacation.

The staff had my number in case of an emergency. Emails could wait until I stopped at a gas station or when I was in my hotel room each night. They'd be fine without me for a couple weeks, right? Besides a natural disaster or fire, I could handle almost any emergency remotely.

The resort ran like a well-oiled machine, at least when I was behind the wheel. I'd refined processes and procedures, training my subordinates with precision. My capable team could handle anything that came up for two weeks. As long as no one quit.

Oh God, please don't let anyone quit. My heart thumped again. Was this how parents felt when they sent their children off to college? No wonder mothers cried and fathers loitered on drop-off day. It was disquieting.

This resort was my baby. My everything. I worked ten-hour days, six days per week. I came in every other Sunday morning to approve payroll and stayed late on Tuesday nights to meet with the chef and go over his upcoming meal plan.

We were heading into the peak summer season and I actually didn't have time for a road trip across the Pacific Northwest. *Maybe I should cancel.*

Except I truly, desperately, achingly *needed* this trip.

Because if I had to see Cash today after he'd spent the past two nights away from home and in a woman's bed, I'd claw my eyes out. Since I really loved my eyes and the ability to see, I had to get some space.

Eight hundred and thirty-one miles of space, to be exact.

That was how far it was to Heron Beach, Oregon, from Clear River, Montana.

After one last scroll through my email, I shut down my computer, stuffing the laptop along with my phone in my tote. The two pens beside my planner—one red for employee-related tasks, one blue for guest activities—were put into their designated slot in my drawer. The paper clip that was attempting to escape a contract was straightened. The sticky note I'd used for this morning's checklist was crumpled and tossed in the trash. Then I ran my hand over the back of my executive chair, pushing it under the oak desk.

The clock beside my wall of bookshelves showed I had ten minutes until eight, when I was due at Gemma's to pick up the Cadillac. I'd been working since five but this nagging feeling that I was forgetting something made me wish I'd come in at four.

I took one last glance at my tidy desk and my eyes caught on the single framed picture I kept beside the phone. It was of me standing with the Greers. As an honorary member of their family, they'd invited—ordered—me to show up on picture day seven years ago. This was the family photo currently on the resort's website and in its brochures.

Now that Easton and Gemma were engaged and having a baby, I suspected we'd be taking a new photo soon. But this one would always be a favorite. Maybe because it was from so long ago.

Everyone looked the same, more or less. Jake and Carol, the ranch's founders, had a few more wrinkles these days. Their son, JR, and his wife, Liddy, had both retired. Easton smiled more since he'd fallen in love with Gemma.

But Cash looked exactly the same. Handsome with his devilish grin and bright hazel eyes that reminded me of sunshine streaming through a forest's leaves.

He had his arm around my shoulders as he smiled straight ahead at the camera. Maybe the reason I loved this picture so much was because it was easy to look at it and pretend that we were every bit the loving, happy couple we appeared to be.

Except Cash had been my friend, and only my friend, for twelve years. We'd met early on in my career at the resort, when I'd been a housekeeper and living in the staff quarters. He'd come home from college for spring break and the two of us had hit it off over our mutual love for Mountain Dew. In all those years, he'd never once flirted. He'd never once asked me out or led me on.

This ridiculous and epic crush was entirely one-sided.

I put the frame down, face-first, hiding the picture from view. We weren't a couple. We wouldn't *be* a couple. And it was time to let him go.

It was time for a new picture.

"Katherine?" Carol poked her head through my office door. "Oh, good. You're still here."

"Hi." I smiled at my adopted grandmother and the woman I wanted to become. For as long as I lived, I doubted I'd meet anyone with as much fire and spirit as Carol Greer. "What's up?"

The smile on her face was warm and gentle as she crossed the room with an envelope in her hand. Her hair was braided in a long, bright-white rope that draped over her shoulder. She was in a soft flannel shirt tucked into a pair of well-worn jeans. The woman had more money than I could even contemplate amassing in my lifetime, and her boots—the ones I'd bought her as a birthday gift five years ago—were scuffed beyond recognition.

"This is for you." She extended the envelope across my desk.

"What is it?" I took it from her, giving it a sideways glance.

She smiled and the crinkles around her brown eyes deepened. "Open it."

I lifted the unsealed flap and pulled out a check she'd folded in half. A check for . . . "Oh my God. Carol."

"It's just a little something from me and Jake to you."

"This is not little." She'd written me a check for ten thousand dollars. "I can't accept this. It's too much."

"Yes, you can and yes, you will. It's a gift. I want you to enjoy this vacation. You haven't taken one in twelve years. Have fun. Spend that money recklessly. Enjoy your time away. We'll have everything here covered."

My eyes stayed glued to the amount. I earned a good

living as the general manager at the Greers' multimillion-dollar resort. My truck was paid for and Cash refused to let me pay rent at the house we shared, so most of my salary went into savings. But seeing the numbers on a computer screen after my bimonthly direct deposit wasn't quite the same. I'd never held a check, *a gift*, for ten. Thousand. Dollars. I forced my gaze from the paper. "Thank you. This is . . . *thank you*."

"You're welcome." She nodded and dug into her jeans pocket, pulling out a quarter and handing it over. "And I have one more thing. It comes with a story."

"Okay." I smiled. Carol's stories were my favorite.

She perched on the edge of my desk. "When I was a kid, my daddy took me on a road trip. It was just for a weekend. We were poor and couldn't afford anything fancy. We loaded up a tent and some sleeping bags and a cooler full of food and set out. My mom was five months pregnant and Dad wanted to do something with just me before my sister was born."

"That's sweet."

"He was a sweet man." There was so much fondness in her voice. I was glad she'd loved her father and sad that she'd lost him. "We played a game. Heads left. Tails right. That's how we decided where to go."

"What a fun idea. Where'd you end up?"

"Not far. I think we spent most of one day driving in circles. But we made it almost all the way to Idaho before the time was up and we had to turn back."

The quarter, pinched between my finger and thumb, glinted as the sun streamed through the windows at my back.

"Don't feel like you need to rush back," she said. "Take two weeks. Take three. Take four. Take the time you need, and if you feel like exploring, flip the coin."

Four weeks? I swallowed a laugh. She'd be lucky if I actually made it the planned two.

I tucked the quarter into my pocket. "Thank you. For the gift. And for sharing your story."

She rounded the desk and put her hands on my shoulders. "We love you, Kat."

"I love you too." I went easily into her arms, closing my eyes and taking a long breath. She smelled of wind and earth and lilac blooms, sweet, but strong and free.

"Miss you already."

"You too." I gave her one last long squeeze, then let her go to heft my tote over a shoulder. "Call me if you need anything. Annabeth has a list of everything that needs to be done for the guests and Easton has the excursion schedule—"

"Honey, did you forget who built this resort from the ground up?" Carol laughed, taking my elbow and steering me for the door. "We'll manage."

"I know." I sighed. "Sorry. I don't mean to be disrespectful. I just feel . . . guilty."

"Because you work too hard. And I know you don't

mean to be disrespectful. But this is your chance to disconnect. Trust me. We'll be fine."

"Okay." I leaned into her, taking one last glance over my shoulder at the windows and view beyond.

I loved this office. I loved the woman I was in this office. Confident. Commanding. Successful. Never in my wildest dreams would I have thought I'd grow up to be the woman in the corner office, running one of Montana's premier, luxury ranch resorts.

Green meadows blanketed the valley bordered by rolling, tree-covered hills. The mountains in the distance stood tall and blue. There was snow on their peaks, the white caps shining under the brilliant morning sky.

It was captivating and bold. Guests from all over the world came to stay here because the landscape was wholly enchanting. There was a reason why I hadn't taken a vacation in years. When you lived in paradise, why leave?

This trip of mine wasn't out of wanderlust. It was a necessary escape. The mental image of Cash canoodling with Dany, the surprise girlfriend, at Friday night's family dinner was enough to make me scream.

Carol escorted me out of my office, flipping off the light as we passed the threshold. She probably felt my itching desire to go back in and check my planner just one more time, so she kept her arm looped with mine, leading —dragging—me down the long hallway. Her boots echoed on the floor's wooden planks as we passed the row of empty offices.

This wing of the lodge was mostly offices, storage and two conference rooms for the occasional corporation who sent their executives away for a working retreat. Beneath us was the dining room and five-star kitchen. The guest rooms were on the other end of the lodge and we also had chalets and extravagant tents.

We sold Montana luxury. Our guests came here for a *traditional Western experience*—at least, that was the marketing pitch. Nothing about the Greer resort was traditional. We catered to the uber rich, the celebrities and urban wealthy who wanted to escape reality for a week to go hiking, horseback riding and glamping in Montana.

Our reputation and quality of experience meant we could charge four thousand dollars per night for a lavish, rustic, three-bedroom chalet.

I glanced at Annabeth's office as we passed, my heart sinking to see it dark and empty. I was late to meet Gemma but I would have felt better had I touched base with at least one employee before leaving.

Besides the kitchen staff who'd been here since six, most of my employees wouldn't arrive until eight thirty. JR's office was across from mine, and while technically retired, he liked to come in around eleven each day, giving him plenty of time for one last cup of coffee before raiding the kitchen for lunch.

"I went through the menu for the next two weeks, but when JR comes in today, will you ask him to check in regularly? Chef Wong will go off menu if someone isn't keeping tabs."

The man was a brilliant chef who we'd hired from New York, but he forgot at times that we weren't in Manhattan and our guests weren't here to try gourmet fusion.

"Yes, we'll make sure he stays on menu," Carol said as we reached the top of the wide, sweeping staircase that dropped to the lobby.

"And will you remind Annabeth that we have a guest in a wheelchair coming Thursday? It's a little boy with cerebral palsy. They're staying in the Eagle Ridge Chalet and I'd like to have her escort them personally to make sure the arrangement will work."

"Anything else?" Carol side-eyed me.

"Um . . ." Yes. About a million things. "You know what? I'll just email Annabeth from the road."

"Katherine, will you relax?"

"I'm relaxed." I forced a too-wide smile as we reached the lobby. The smell of fresh coffee, bacon, eggs and pancakes filled the air. A couple crossed the foyer, headed for the dining room. "Good morning."

They both smiled and returned my greeting before disappearing to get breakfast.

"Shoot." I slipped my arm free of Carol's and rushed to the front desk, where the receptionist's stool was empty. "I forgot to tell Chef Wong about a party coming next week. They requested a special prime rib dinner, which shouldn't be a problem, but I don't want him to forget."

"Which reservation?" Carol asked, appearing at my side.

"Boyd. They'll be in the Grizzly Chalet."

"Okay." She waved me off and grabbed a pen to scribble on a sticky note. "I'll take care of it."

"I can just buzz into the kitchen—"

"Katherine Gates." She pinned me with a stare normally reserved for her grandsons, son or husband. "I will see you in two weeks."

"Fine," I muttered. "I'm going. I'll call and check—"

"You will do no such thing." She planted her hands on her hips. "Don't call."

"But—"

"Kat, take this vacation. It's for your own good."

I fought a cringe, despising those words.

Carol's voice gentled and the pleading in her eyes made me hold my breath. "Let's not pretend I don't know the reason why you decided to take this whirlwind trip. Cash showed up at family dinner with a woman and . . . I get it. I think it's a brilliant idea for you to get away."

I had too much stubborn pride to confess that I was in love with my best friend. But I'd been a fool to think Carol hadn't noticed my feelings for her grandson. I'd loved Cash for years. Did all of the Greers know? Did they share pitiful glances behind my back?

Our poor Kat, stuck in the friend zone for life.

I swallowed a groan.

"Go." She put her hand on my arm. "When I told you to take some time, I meant it. You need to get away from here and decide if this is really the life you want."

"What are you saying?" Why wouldn't I want this life?

"We love you. You are a part of our family, whether you live and work here or not. But you need to get away from here. Breathe. Think. Let him go."

Ouch. Hadn't I thought the exact same thing myself? So why did it hurt so much to hear from someone else?

"I don't want you spending your life waiting," she said.

The lump in my throat made it impossible to speak, so I nodded and stretched a tight smile across my face.

"Go." She kissed my cheek. "Think it over. I would hate to lose you, but I would hate for you to stay here and be unhappy even more."

I walked away from the desk, my head spinning. Why did it feel like I'd just been kicked out? Why did it feel like I'd just been given an ultimatum?

Get over Cash or go somewhere he's not.

Carol had good intentions and I believed that she was looking out for me. She didn't want me to suffer here while he moved on with his life. I didn't want that for myself.

But it was a stark reminder of the truth. I wasn't a Greer. I was the guest in the family photo.

Cash was the Greer, and she wasn't losing her grandson.

My truck was waiting outside the lodge, parked in front of a hitching post we used for space markers. I climbed inside and sucked in a deep breath, fighting the urge to cry.

Part of me wanted to shove my head in the dirt and pretend like this wasn't an issue. After all, I'd been practicing that move for years. I could go about my work, enjoy my simple life and drown the feelings I'd been harboring for a decade in work and denial.

But that wasn't working out so well for me, was it? I'd arrived at a crossroads and maybe after eight hundred and thirty-one miles, I'd know which path to take.

I sucked in another deep breath, then started the truck and reversed out of my space. The gravel road that wound from the lodge to the highway was damp from last night's rain shower, and the grass along the drive glistened. My tires didn't kick up the normal cloud of dust as I drove, giving me a clear view of the imposing lodge through the rearview mirror.

Its logs had been stained a dark, reddish brown. The towering peak of the eaves was nearly as tall as the hundred-year-old evergreens that clustered around the structure.

That building was home. It was my sanctuary. And with every turn of my wheels, I felt it slipping through my grasp. As the lodge grew smaller and smaller in the distance, I was more and more certain I wouldn't see it again.

"You're being silly," I singsonged to myself, aiming my gaze straight ahead.

This was only a vacation. I'd be back in two weeks or less, my feelings for Cash under control. Plus, I had a ten-thousand-dollar check in my pocket.

The frugal girl who'd once begged for spare change demanded it go into savings. But the woman who rarely splurged on herself pictured spa treatments and mono-grammed robes and a shopping spree.

A wave of excitement rushed through my veins, swirling with my nerves in a heady mix of anticipation.

Oregon, here I come.

I'd be on my way as soon as I picked up the car.

Eight hundred and thirty-one miles. And twenty-five cents in my pocket.

Maybe Carol had been onto something. I had no schedule. Though I wasn't going to spend three or four weeks on the road, maybe I needed to force myself to spend two. Fourteen days was plenty of time to get to Oregon and hop on a plane home. It was plenty of time to spend an extra day or two exploring.

The coin in my pocket begged to be flipped.

Heads left. Tails right.

I smiled, anxious to pick up the Cadillac and sit behind the wheel. One more stop, then I was gone.

One more stop, then I'd take this trip by quarter miles.

CHAPTER TWO

KATHERINE

I pulled into Gemma and Easton's driveway just as my beautiful, pregnant friend came out the front door.

"Morning," I called as I got out of my truck.

"Hey." She waved me up the porch. "Easton should be back soon with the car."

"Where did he take it?" I was anxious to get on the road.

"To fill it up."

I frowned as I reached the top step. "I know how to get gas."

"Oh, I didn't send him away for you. He was driving me crazy, hovering over my every move, so I kicked him out."

I giggled. "How are you today?"

"Good." She smiled, leading me to the porch swing. "How are you?"

"Nervous," I admitted. "I haven't taken a trip in a long time."

"You'll love it." She stroked her belly as I sat at her side, her eyes wandering over the view ahead.

"Yeah, I think I will. It was a good idea."

"Thank you." She shimmied with pride. "I have my moments."

Like the other Greer homes on the property, Easton and Gemma's place was rustic and refined. The dark-stained exterior was broken by shiny, glimmering windows. The meadows surrounding their place were blooming with spring flowers. A deer and her fawn inched out from a copse of cottonwood trees, their noses bent to the grass and their ears raised at attention.

We sat on the swing, rocking gently in the cool, crisp morning air. I tugged the sleeves of my sweater over my chilly knuckles as Gemma shoved her sleeves above her elbows. For the past month of her pregnancy, she'd cursed often how it was *so damn hot*.

"Any word from your private investigator on Aria?"

"He emailed me last night and said she's still in Heron Beach." Gemma shifted to take a sticky note from her pocket. "Here's her address and the name of the hotel where she works."

I took the note and stuffed it into my pocket. "God, this is crazy."

"Maybe."

"What if she doesn't want to see me?"

Gemma scoffed. "Please. This is Aria we're talking about. She'll hug you so hard it'll probably crack a rib."

I smiled. "True."

It was going to be strange seeing Aria after all these years. I could still see her and her sister, Clara, standing at the bus station, waving as Gemma, Londyn and I boarded a Greyhound destined for Montana. Clara had been crying while Aria had laughed, flipping us off for leaving them behind.

"Do you think she'll take the car to California?" I asked.

Gemma shrugged. "I don't know. Maybe. But if not, that's okay. Come home and Easton and I will take it after the baby's born."

On cue, a shiny red Cadillac appeared on the gravel lane ahead.

This was it. That was my ride. Damn, I was nervous. About leaving. About driving. About everything. When had I become this cowardly recluse?

I'd grown up in Temecula, California. Though the city at large appealed, my childhood had not. I hadn't grown up in a dreamy, suburban home with a white picket fence and a goldendoodle named Rover. My youth had been a nightmare. At sixteen, I'd run away from home to live in a junkyard with five other teenagers who'd each survived nightmares of their own, Gemma included.

She'd been my roommate in the junkyard. The two of us had shared a makeshift tent, while Aria and Clara had

19

lived in an old delivery van, and Londyn and Karson had turned a rusted 1969 Cadillac DeVille convertible into a home.

The very car that bounced and bumped our way.

"Did you call Londyn?" I asked Gemma.

"I did. And she thinks my idea is brilliant too. She loves that her car is bringing us all together."

"Me too."

As we'd grown up, I'd lost touch with my junkyard friends. Gemma, Londyn and I had come to Montana for jobs at the resort, but they hadn't lasted long. Londyn only four months, Gemma eight. They'd both landed in Boston and we'd gone years without talking until one day last fall, Gemma had shown up at the resort out of the blue, driving a Cadillac.

Londyn had rescued her Cadillac from the junkyard and she'd had it completely restored. It was a piece of classic Americana. A showstopper. She'd set out in that Cadillac on a journey of her own, to find a new life. After she had, she'd given the car to Gemma, urging her to take her own trip.

Now it was my turn behind the wheel.

"Have you, um, talked to Cash?" Gemma asked. "About the trip?"

"No. He didn't come home on Friday." Or last night.

Every Friday night, the Greers had a family dinner at Carol and Jake's home. It was a long-standing tradition, and much like the family photo, I'd been invited—

expected—to attend. Maybe my last name wasn't Greer, but from the outside, you'd never know.

I'd cherished that invitation and rarely missed a Friday.

When Gemma had arrived, they'd invited her too. They'd pulled her into their family without hesitation, but besides us, the unspoken rule was that dinner was not for others.

Easton, Cash and I didn't bring dates to family dinner because unless it was serious, you came alone. None of us had ever been in a serious enough relationship to warrant a family dinner introduction.

Or so I'd thought.

Last Friday, Cash had brought Dany, a pretty blonde I'd known for years, to dinner. Her family was from this area and they had their own ranch outside of Clear River. Her father served with me on the town council and always bragged about how much Dany loved being a nurse in Missoula, the closest city, located forty miles away.

All through dinner, Cash had been enamored with Dany. Laughing. Whispering. Touching.

It had broken my heart. Just like it had broken my heart knowing he'd spent the weekend with her while I'd been home alone, crying into a pint of ice cream because the man I'd loved for years would only ever see me as Kat, his unofficial sister.

"I'm pathetic," I whispered.

"No, you're not." Gemma took my hand. "He's an idiot."

"No, he's not."

Cash Greer was a good man. He loved working with horses. He loved his family. He loved this ranch.

He just didn't love me.

Easton pulled the Cadillac into the space beside my truck and Gemma pushed herself out of the swing, leading with her belly. My hands shook as I stood, shifting weight from one foot to the other as Easton climbed out of the driver's seat. The cherry-red paint on the Cadillac's hood was polished to a shine. Its chrome fender gleamed. It was one hell of a sight.

And for the next two weeks, it was mine.

I scrambled down the porch steps, greeting Easton as I went to the truck to unload my things. The sooner I got out of here, the sooner I would relax. I went to lift my caramel suitcase and move it to the Cadillac's trunk, but Easton was there to do it for me.

"Just this?" Easton asked.

"And my purse." I grabbed it from the truck's front seat and took it to the Cadillac. "Thanks for taking care of everything. Call me if something comes up, okay?"

Easton slammed the trunk closed, my suitcase safely stowed. "I will."

While Carol had insisted on handling everything on her own, Easton wouldn't be as insistent on shutting me out. When things weren't running smoothly at the resort, it only caused him stress, and when Easton was stressed, he wasn't quiet about it.

The Greers had set up their business in two parts—the ranch and the resort. Both worked closely in tandem with one another, and while I managed the resort, Easton managed the ranch.

With thousands of acres to manage and maintain, he didn't have time to dabble in guest services, nor did he have the desire. He would rather stay in his office in the stables than in the lodge with a waiting smile for any guest.

As I focused my daily efforts on hospitality, Easton was busy overseeing all operations concerning the land itself and the livestock. He and his staff ensured pastures were fenced and free of noxious weeds. They managed the cattle herd and the horses. When my guests wanted to go on a trail ride, Easton's crew led the excursion. From hikes to wagon rides to bonfires to guided hunting experiences, his team handled anything outdoors.

If an activity involved a pillow, fork or confirmation number, it fell under my domain. When JR had retired and I'd been promoted to manager four years ago, the two of us had developed a system. We counted on each other for honesty and open lines of communication. Our relationship was built on trust.

If there was a disaster, Easton would call, and knowing that settled some nerves about this vacation.

"Have fun," Gemma said, settling into Easton's side. "Don't worry about things here."

I nodded. "I'll try."

"Got your Triple A card?" Easton asked.

"Uh, no." Why would I have Triple A? I hadn't gone anywhere in years so why would I need roadside insurance? "But I have a phone."

He frowned. "What if you get a flat?"

"Then I'll change it and finally put the hours of practice you made me endure to good use."

Jake and JR had taken shifts teaching me how to drive. They hadn't been able to believe that I'd come to Montana at eighteen and never been behind a wheel. But it was Easton I'd called when I'd gotten my first—and only—flat tire on a trip to Missoula. We'd come home and for the next week, he'd made me change one tire a day until he was sure I had it mastered.

Easton was the oldest of the Greer sons and the closest thing I had to a big brother. He was overprotective and mildly annoying, but kind. When Gemma, Londyn and I had come to the ranch from the junkyard, he'd been working on the ranch, having already finished college. He was handsome and rugged, but he was too broody and serious for my taste. Besides, his heart had been Gemma's for a long, long time.

They were the perfect pair. Her sass and steel mellowed him. He tamed her wild nature and gave her roots.

They would be difficult to be around if I didn't love them both so much.

"Do you want some cookies for the road?" Gemma asked, looking down the gravel road. "I made some last night."

"No, that's okay. I think I'll just get going."

"But are you sure? You might get hungry." Before I could protest again, she held up a finger and walked toward the house.

"Tell me these aren't an experimental batch," I said to Easton once she was out of earshot.

Gemma had been *enhancing* a standard chocolate chip cookie recipe for the past month. Every few days, she'd come to my office with a half dozen for me to sample. When she'd brought in the batch with raisins and pistachios, I'd told her I was on a new diet, no sugar allowed.

"No," Easton said. "These are actually pretty good."

Gemma emerged a minute later with a zippered plastic bag stuffed with cookies. She took each step slowly, her eyes once again searching the road as she came to my side.

I glanced over my shoulder but the lane was empty. "What?"

"Nothing." She handed me the cookies. "I thought I saw a deer."

"Ah." I nodded. "Okay. Time to get going."

The quarter in my pocket was getting heavier and I was anxious to give it a flip.

Gemma pulled me in for a hug. "I wish I could go with you."

"Me too." I held her tighter, her baby belly requiring me to stand on my tiptoes to get over the bump. "Rest, okay?"

"Yeah," she muttered.

At her prenatal checkup on Friday, the doctor had put her on activity rest, concerned with her blood pressure. Until their baby boy was born in a couple months, she was to *relax*. Gemma didn't actually know what that word meant so I suspected the next two months would be entertaining at the very least.

In all the years I'd known Gemma, she'd never stopped moving. Her ambitions were unparalleled.

Cash was that way, in a state of perpetual motion. Unless we were watching a movie together, he always had something to do, whether it be an odd job around the house or something with a horse at the stables. Then again, maybe I just saw him as busy because we shared a home.

The idea that he hadn't been home made my heart twist.

Was he still with her? Would he even notice I was gone? Or would he take this opportunity to fuck his girl-friend on our living room couch?

Five years ago, I'd moved in with Cash. At the time, I'd been living in the staff quarters—a dormitory of sorts for the single, young, seasonal employees who didn't have their own home in the area, complete with cramped rooms and communal bathrooms. Not that I was picky. I'd spent years in a dirty junkyard, and my childhood home before that hadn't been much better.

Carol and Jake had just built a new house in the foothills, their retirement home, and Cash had been living in their old home, alone with nearly three thousand square feet and two extra bedrooms.

I'd accepted his invitation immediately. Living with Cash was easy. Comfortable. We talked every morning over coffee and cereal. We ate dinner together each night. He was my best friend. My confidant. My companion.

Five years, and in that time, he'd never once disappeared to a woman's bed. Hell, he hadn't even bothered to tell me he had a girlfriend.

A trip to Oregon and back was just what I needed to erase the sting of his silence.

"Be careful," Easton said, giving me a hug goodbye.

"I will." I stepped to the door, ready to get in, when the sound of a diesel engine caught my ear. My gaze flicked to the road as a truck appeared.

Shit. That was Cash's truck.

Call it petty, but I'd hoped to give him a dose of his own by keeping this trip of mine a secret.

The urge to hop in the Cadillac tempted me toward the driver's seat. But damn my feet, they stayed rooted in place, waiting as he eased into the empty space beside my truck in the driveway.

Had Gemma been waiting for him? Was that why she'd been looking down the road?

No. No way. This trip was her idea. She'd been at dinner on Friday night when Cash had arrived with Dany. Gemma knew how hard it had been for me to see him with another woman. This trip had been her idea. She'd suggested I take the Cadillac, get some distance and give my heart a chance to heal.

Though she didn't look surprised as he shut off his truck and stepped out. No, she looked . . . guilty.

Cash sauntered over wearing the same clothes he'd had on Friday night.

Nice. That was exactly what I needed—a reminder that he'd been sleeping somewhere other than his own damn bed.

"Hey." His voice was gravelly and rough, like he'd just woken up.

It was the voice that made my knees weak every morning when he shuffled into the kitchen in search of coffee. His dark hair would be sticking out in all directions. He'd be wearing only a low-slung pair of pajama pants, his broad, naked chest and washboard abs on full display.

Was that where things had gone wrong? Maybe I shouldn't have moved in with Cash. Any hot-blooded woman would fall for a sexy cowboy with a strong, stubbled jaw and a sleepy, devilish smile.

Convincing myself that living together was the problem might have been plausible if this crush of mine hadn't started years before we'd ever shared a roof.

My feelings for Cash had grown like the evergreens, ring by ring until the trunk was so massive I couldn't wrap my arms around it.

Still, when I got back, I was moving out. If I managed to get my feelings under control, great. Even then, I didn't want to hear Cash's bedsprings squeak when he let Dany sleep over.

I'd never liked that girl. She was too perfect, with her satin blond hair and perpetual smile.

Dany. Ugh. My lip curled.

"What?" he asked, stopping in front of me, his gaze on my scowl.

"Nothing." I waved it off.

"How'd it go?" Easton asked Cash.

Really? Couldn't they do the play-by-play of Cash's weekend spent screwing his girlfriend *after* I left?

Cash shrugged. "Meh."

Meh? I guess Dany wasn't so perfect after all. It cheered me up a smidge to know she was mediocre in bed.

"Did you see the lion?" Easton asked.

Wait. What? "Lion? We have a lion?"

Cash nodded. "Gemma said she saw a mountain lion at the expansion property."

"When?" My eyes bugged out. "Why didn't you tell me?"

"Didn't I?" She twirled a lock of her chocolate-brown hair. "Huh. I thought I did. Pregnancy brain is no joke."

I narrowed my stare but she refused to make eye contact.

"We need to change activities," I said, instantly switching to crisis management mode. "We can't have guests out hiking if there is a lion in the area. Should we call that guy? What was his name? The one with the hound dogs?" My vacation had just taken a hiatus, but I couldn't leave guests at risk. "I'll go to the office and call the game warden."

"Hold up." Easton raised his hand, stopping me before I could race to my truck, and looked to Cash. "Did you see any signs?"

He shook his head. "Not a sign. I hiked all over, looking for paw prints or scat. Didn't see a thing."

"When?" I asked.

"Where do you think I've been for the past two nights?"

My heart stopped. He hadn't been with Dany.

"Glad you missed me at home. Did you watch our Netflix show?"

Yes, I had watched the show we'd been binging, but I hadn't felt guilty about it until now. "Uh . . ."

"I knew it." He frowned. "Watching our show without me, eating my popcorn while I was sleeping in the back of my goddamn truck, trying to find this mysterious lion."

He hadn't been with Dany. My spirits soared like a kite on the wind, flying into the open blue sky. But before I got carried away, I tugged them back in. Cash still had a girlfriend. They hadn't had a tryst this weekend, but it was only a matter of time. He had a girlfriend. And I was only his best friend.

"Gem, are you sure you saw a lion?" Cash asked.

She lifted a shoulder. "I thought so. It was big but pretty far away. Maybe it was a coyote."

A coyote. A toddler could tell the difference between a mountain lion and a coyote even at a distance. What was she up to?

I planted my hands on my hips and willed Gemma to look at me. She was six inches taller than my five one and she kept her gaze carefully lifted above my head. With Easton and Cash both standing inches above six feet, I was by far the smallest in the group.

The runt.

I hated being short. I squared my shoulders and lengthened my spine, demanding attention. Maybe I was short in stature but that didn't mean I didn't have my own force. "What's going on, Gemma?"

"What?" She feigned innocence. "I thought I saw a mountain lion."

Easton dropped his gaze to his boots, shuffling and kicking at a rock on the gravel driveway. That asshole had never been a good liar.

Regardless of their motives for this lion stunt, at the moment, I could hug them both. Cash and Dany were an inevitability that I'd have to deal with. But for today, I'd get to leave for my trip and not have mental images of them together clouding my windshield.

Gemma finally met my gaze and gave me a small smile.

I mouthed, "Thank you."

She winked.

"Are you guys taking the Cadillac out today?" Cash asked Easton, covering a yawn with his fist.

I shook my head, willing Gemma to keep her mouth shut. She did. It was Easton who I should have kicked in the knee.

"Actually, Katherine's taking a vacation," he said.

"What?" Cash asked at the same time I shot Easton a glare.

So much for disappearing. Part of the reason I hadn't wanted to tell Cash about this was to punish him. The other part was because he wasn't the only overprotective Greer in the mix.

"Where are you going? Why? When?" Cash asked, crowding me with that imposing body. It was a classic Greer intimidation tactic and once upon a time, it would have worked. But I'd become immune to the way they hovered and glowered to get their way.

I was a woman in charge. After all, I'd been taking notes from Carol for years.

I poked a finger in his chest, sending him back a step, and held up my chin. "Today. And I'm not sure exactly where I'm going yet."

"Huh?" Gemma asked at the same time Easton said, "I thought you were going to Oregon."

"Yes, eventually I'll get to Oregon. But Carol stopped by this morning and gave me an idea. So I'm going to explore before I go see Aria. I'm going to flip a coin and see where it takes me."

Easton shook his head, crossing his arms over his chest. "That's dangerous."

"But you're fine with me driving to Oregon? It's the same trip with a few more turns along the way."

"It's different."

"No, it's not." I was still going on a trip. Alone.

"Well, I love it," Gemma declared.

"Didn't Grandma do that with her dad once?" Cash rubbed the beard he'd grown over the past month.

"Yes, she did."

He hummed, his eyes darting to Easton and Gemma's house. "Mind if I use your bathroom?"

"Go for it." Easton waved him inside.

Cash squeezed my shoulder as he walked past. "Don't leave yet."

"Okay." I'd expected some sort of objection to this trip, but maybe he'd hug me goodbye and that would be the end of it. That was a good thing, right? If Cash wasn't worrying about me, thinking about me, then I could go and attempt to not think about him.

"I don't think this is a good idea," Easton said.

"I think it's great." Gemma jabbed her elbow into his ribs, hissing, "Be supportive."

Easton's shoulders fell. "Drive careful."

"I will." I gave him one last hug, then did the same with Gemma.

Easton held the driver's side door open as I slid behind the Cadillac's smooth, white steering wheel.

The matching leather seat wrapped me in a buttery hug as I inched it forward so my feet would touch the pedals. The interior was impeccable and smelled like polish and pine—Easton's doing, no doubt. When I turned the key, the engine purred. The moment the temperature was above seventy, I was lowering the convertible top and driving with the wind in my sable hair.

This Cadillac was a dream. Londyn had done the restoration right, maintaining the car's classic appearance while enriching it with modern touches. It was hard to believe this was the same car that had been parked beside Gemma's and my tent. The rust and wear were gone. The doors closed without squeaks. The windows were uncracked.

It was a masterpiece.

Easton pushed the door closed, shutting me inside.

I rolled down the window and let my palms rest on the wheel, excitement bubbling through my fingertips.

"I love this quarter flip," Gemma said, crouching as low as she could next to the window. "I wish I could go with you."

"Next time." I smiled as Cash emerged through their front door. I did a double take as he jogged down the porch stairs.

Why was he carrying a backpack?

Cash clapped Easton on the shoulder before rounding the hood toward the passenger side. He flung the door open and bent in half, sliding into the seat.

"What are you doing?" I asked.

He answered by shutting his door and buckling his seat belt.

"Cash," I warned.

"Hand over the quarter." He held out his hand. "I'll flip the coin."

CHAPTER THREE

CASH

I needed a shower and a nap, in that order, but I doubted I'd get either.

"Where are you going?" I asked as Katherine took a right on the highway. "I thought heads was left."

I had flipped heads, hadn't I? I was nearly delirious after two sleepless nights in the backseat of my truck.

Camping out had been fun in my teens and twenties, but damn it, I was thirty years old and wanted to sleep in a bed. The next time Gemma confused a mountain lion with a coyote or a grizzly bear with a Black Angus bull, I was making Easton track the animal.

"We're going home," Kat said.

"Mind if I hop in the shower before we take off?"

"There's no we." She shook her head. "I'm dropping you off."

"Didn't we just have this conversation?"

Kat had tried to kick me out of the Cadillac but I hadn't budged. We'd sat in Easton's driveway long enough that both he and Gemma had given up observing the argument and had retreated inside. When Kat had finally reversed away from Easton's place, I'd thought she'd consented. I should have known better.

Once, I'd bought her a coffee mug that read, *Though she be but little, she is fierce.*

"You're not coming with me, Cash."

"You're not going alone, Kat."

"Yes, I am." Her nostrils flared and her face was turning this violent shade of red that meant soon she'd be spewing profanities and calling me every dirty name in her arsenal. But Kat could yell and rant and curse me up one side and down the other.

There was no way I was letting her drive aimlessly around the country alone.

It wasn't safe. It wasn't smart. And it sure as fuck wasn't happening.

"I don't want you along," she barked.

"Tough shit, sweetheart. I'm coming."

"No, you're not." Her foot jammed the accelerator, jolting me into the seat. "Jackass."

The names would get more creative, but unless she developed superhuman strength in the next five minutes, there was no way she'd be able to haul me out of this car.

I'd stolen some clothes from Easton's closet—thankfully we were the same size—and some toiletries from their guest bathroom. After Gemma had moved in with him, she'd stocked the place with the essentials. I'd taken the liberty of acquiring a toothbrush, toothpaste and bottle of shampoo.

"You're a dickhead," Kat muttered.

"I know." I relaxed deeper into the seat and closed my eyes. The Cadillac was surprisingly comfortable, and though it wasn't as good as a bed, I'd survive. Twisting and turning, I shifted until my head was propped up between the seat and the door. "Give me a couple hours, then I'll take the next shift to drive."

No response.

I waited five breaths, then cracked an eyelid.

Katherine's mouth was pursed in a hard line and if she didn't let up on the steering wheel, her fingers were going to make permanent indentations.

"Hey." I reached across the cab and brushed my knuckle over her elbow. "Don't be mad."

She jerked her arm away. "Prick."

"I don't want you taking this trip alone. Easton is right. It's dangerous." Too many things could go wrong. There were too many sick fucks in the world. "It's for your own good."

Kat gave me a sneer that would eviscerate most men. "I'm not some hopeless waif who needs your protection."

"I know." Katherine Gates was the strongest, toughest woman I'd ever met. That still didn't mean I was sending her off into the unknown alone. "Then what if I just want a vacation too?"

"Take a vacation."

"I am." I grinned. "With you."

"What about work?"

I scoffed. "Some of us are replaceable."

That got her attention. Some of the fire in her crystal-blue eyes faded. "That's not true. What about the expansion?"

My family was in the middle of expanding our operation to include a state-of-the-art equine breeding and training facility. It would be mine to run with Gemma. When Easton had announced his plans to expand the ranch, she'd invested as a partner.

"Now's the time to leave, before we get busy. Besides, if I'm not there working, Gemma might actually relax." My soon-to-be sister-in-law wasn't one to sit when other people were standing.

Kat sighed. She knew I was right. "Jerk face."

I chuckled and sat up straighter. "Why don't you want me to come along? Are you mad at me or something?"

She'd been noticeably quiet on Friday night at dinner with the family and it wasn't like her to exclude me from anything. It also wasn't like her to arrange for a spontaneous trip without so much as mentioning it to me.

"Kat?" I prompted.

No answer.

Okay, she was mad. "What? What did I do?"

"Nothing," she muttered.

"Then let me come along. Mom and Dad will check on the house. Easton already knows I'm leaving, so he'll rearrange the schedule to cover my shifts."

There were plenty of other guys on his payroll who'd be happy to lead the guided horseback tours and private lessons. I didn't do many of those these days anyway with work ramping up at the training facility.

"Please?" I begged.

"What about Dany?" Kat asked. "Won't she get the wrong idea?"

"Nah." I shifted in my seat, slumping down so far my knees jammed into the glove box. "We called it off on Friday."

The car jerked to the side.

"Whoa." I sat up and glanced behind us. "What was that?"

"Uh . . . gopher."

She swerved to miss them. I swerved to kill. The pests would be running around from now until the end of summer, digging holes in our pastures for the cattle and horses to step in.

The turnoff to our place approached and Katherine slowed the car, easing us off the highway. *Damn it.* She wasn't making this easy.

Well, she wasn't the only stubborn one in the car. She could park at home for hours and I'd just take my nap until she realized, whether she liked it or not, I was going on this trip.

She wasn't the only one who craved a spontaneous vacation. These past few months had been exhausting. Planning at the training facility was going well and the construction crew was slated to break ground within the month.

But working with family—my family in particular—was tough. Everyone had a different opinion.

We need twenty stables. No, we need thirty.

We should hire a separate staff. No, we should utilize the existing hands.

Let's only buy colts this first year. No, we should buy fillies.

There were days when I held up my hands, said fuck it and disappeared to the arena to work with the horses.

Ultimately, how we ran the facility was my decision. But I wanted to let my family feel comfortable expressing their point of view. I valued their experience and input, even when it was overwhelming.

A vacation to let it breathe for a week or two sounded damn nice.

I wasn't sure how Easton did it with the ranch. No wonder he'd been so frustrated these past few years. If not for Gemma, he might have blown a fuse.

But I didn't have a beautiful woman to come home to at night. Well, except Kat. When I needed to vent, she'd always lend an ear. She'd find a way to make me laugh.

Not that I wasn't grateful for this new opportunity. The training facility had been Easton's idea. He knew my talents with horses were wasted on guest excursions and routine ranch work. When this facility opened, if we could just get it running, it would be a dream.

But we had to get it open first.

A road trip with my best friend might save my sanity.

"So, um . . . what happened with Dany?" she asked, the car's wheels crunching on the gravel road as we rolled past a green meadow on the way home.

"We got in the stupidest damn fight." I shook my head, still unable to believe we'd gone from *I adore you, Cash* to *I fucking hate you, asshole* in a span of ten minutes.

"About what?"

"You." I blew out a deep breath. "She didn't like that we lived together."

Kat looked over, her mouth falling open. "Why? Did she, uh, say something specific?"

"No. Just that she didn't like that I had a female roommate."

"Oh."

"Whatever." She wasn't who I'd thought she was anyway. It was no loss.

I'd invited Dany over on Friday night but she'd muttered some comment about not being Kat's biggest fan. How could anyone not like Kat? She was awesome. Funny and smart. She was kind to animals and people alike and as far as I knew, she'd been nothing but polite to Dany.

But what the fuck did I know about women? Our argument had escalated quickly. I'd taken Kat's side. She'd gotten defensive. When Easton had called and told me about the mountain lion, I'd been more than happy to cut the night with Dany short. And I hadn't minded seeing her taillights drive off my ranch.

If I was being honest with myself, I hadn't liked her much. She was a bit shallow for my taste. Too soft. We would have eventually killed each other. But I hadn't dated in a while—a long while—and she was pretty, on the outside. Thankfully, I'd dodged a bullet. Hell, we hadn't even slept together.

"Sorry," Katherine whispered. "You liked her."

"Meh. We only went out twice."

A crease formed between her eyebrows. "But you brought her to family dinner."

"It was just dinner." A dinner I didn't have to cook.

"I thought . . . never mind." She waved it off.

"Thought what?"

"Just that you were more serious if you'd bring her to family dinner."

There was an unspoken rule that Friday dinners were for family members only. Why I'd thought bringing Dany would be a good idea, I wasn't sure. Maybe I'd wanted to see if she could cut it. Stick out my grandmother's scrutiny and laugh at the Greer family inside jokes.

Dany had survived that like a champ. It was my friendship with Kat that had sent her running. *Women.*

43

My guy friends had no problem playing second fiddle to my female best friend. I wouldn't tell Kat this, but Dany hadn't been the first almost girlfriend intimidated by her position in my life.

But like I'd done before, I'd made the easy choice.

Kat.

She let me tease her and wasn't afraid to throw it back. She listened without judgment. I'd take her friendship any day over a lousy lay and relationship drama.

"Oh." Kat kept her eyes on the road, shaking her head.

"It's no loss," I said with a shrug.

Our house came into view down the road. The driveway was empty since both our trucks were at Easton's. My bed was inside that house. My shower. Both were tempting.

But not as tempting as this trip. When was the last time either of us had taken a vacation?

"Let me come with you," I said. "Please?"

She pulled into the driveway, parking in front of the garage. Then she shoved the Cadillac in park and looked over, studying my face.

Katherine's long, dark hair was curled today. Normally she left it straight and tied in a ponytail, but this morning it swirled in soft waves past her shoulders. She'd forgotten sunglasses and the sun caught the blue in her eyes, turning them into sapphire jewels.

"Go take a shower," she said. "You stink."

"Are you going to be here when I come out?"

44

"Depends. You have to agree, right now, not to touch the radio."

She hated music when we were driving. Something about wanting to hear the wheels on the road and enjoy the quiet. It had never bothered me because when we went on trips to Missoula or drove around the ranch, we talked. I didn't need the radio when she was there to keep me company.

I grinned. "Wouldn't dream of it."

———

"HERE." I handed Kat a sunglasses case I'd swiped on my way out of the house.

She kept one hand on the wheel as she pried it open with the other, revealing a pair of mirrored Oakleys. "What are these for?"

"Just because." The last time I'd been in Missoula, I'd stopped at the mall to buy myself a new pair. I'd grabbed those for Kat too, thinking she'd like them. The woman was always losing her sunglasses.

She ran her finger over the frames, staring at them for a long moment before turning to me with a smile that didn't quite reach her eyes. She looked almost sad as she said, "Thanks."

"You're welcome." I winked, hoping to cheer her up. "Should we take a bet on if you have those when we get home?"

Kat rolled her eyes and slid them on.

After my two-minute shower, I'd packed a bag of my own clothes and my own toothbrush for the trip. True to her word, Kat had been waiting for me in the car, her fingers flying over the screen of her phone, probably shooting off a string of last-minute emails.

I rolled down the window, letting the air dry my damp hair as Kat pulled onto the highway. "How's this gonna go?"

She shrugged, speeding up to seventy. "I don't know. I guess when we get to the next place we feel like flipping the coin, we'll flip it."

"But we need to end up in Oregon."

"Yep. We're taking the Cadillac to Heron Beach. To Aria."

Aria. How did I know that name? I played it over and over, trying to place it, then it came to me. "She was one of the kids in the junkyard with you and Gemma, right?"

Kat nodded. "Yes."

"There were six of you?"

"Aria and Clara, the twins. Karson, the only boy who lived there. Then Londyn and Gemma, who came here with me."

I'd been in college when Kat and her friends had arrived, but I'd met them on a trip home for spring break. Grandma had introduced them to me as *her girls.* She'd also warned me to stay away from *her girls* if I wanted to keep breathing.

Carol Greer didn't make idle threats, so I'd stayed away, and after graduation, when I'd returned to the ranch to work, Katherine had been the only *girl* left. By that point, she'd been all but adopted by Grandma and Mom. She was the daughter both of them had always wanted.

Any plans I'd had about hitting on her, asking her out, had flown out the window. And I'd definitely wanted to ask her out.

But it had been for the best. A relationship on the ranch would only lead to disaster. We saw enough of that with the staffers. There'd be flings and hookups, and inevitably, one or both of the involved parties would quit.

I'd resented my family some at first for dictating the type of relationship I had with Kat, limiting my options. Over the years, I'd become grateful. We were too good of friends to risk losing it all. My family had been right to discourage me from pursuing her.

Look how quickly things had fizzled with Dany. Or the women who'd come before. Quality boyfriend material I was not. Friend, I could manage.

And maybe without the other family members around, Kat would finally open up about her past. The two of us talked about anything to do with the ranch. The only topic of conversation Kat ever shied away from was her past.

Years ago, she'd confided in Grandma about her childhood, that she'd run away from home to live in a junkyard, of all the fucking places. The thought made my skin crawl. My Kat, tiny, beautiful, loving Kat, living in trash.

She'd never trusted me with the story and I'd only heard it secondhand.

Grandma and Mom had warned me specifically not to push, that it was Kat's business and not to pry. So I hadn't for years. We'd had plenty of other things to talk about, work and whatever drama was happening with my family or guests at the resort.

But Kat had opened up more since Gemma had returned and it had piqued my curiosity. Kat wasn't forthcoming with details about the life she'd lived before Montana, but she also wasn't running away from the topic like she used to. She must have sprinted from her childhood like a horse bolted from a rattlesnake.

Maybe on this trip she'd feel safe airing some demons.

Maybe I'd finally confess my own secret.

"What's Aria like?" I asked.

"I don't know. I haven't spoken to her since the day we left the junkyard."

"You're sure she's in Oregon?"

"According to Gemma's investigator, she works at a hotel there." Kat shifted to dig a sticky note from her pocket. "The Gallaway."

"And why exactly are we going to see Aria?"

"Because eventually, this car needs to get to Karson in California."

"Then let's go to California."

"No."

I stared at her profile, waiting for an explanation. "Just, no?"

"No, I'd like to find Aria."

"Okay." There was more behind her reasoning than reconnecting with an old friend, but I knew Kat's tones well enough to recognize when a door was about to be slammed in my face. Time to try sneaking through a window. "This was Londyn's car, right?"

"Yeah. She lived in it with Karson. He was the first one at Lou's and kind of made it our place."

"Wait. Who's Lou?"

"The owner of the junkyard. I told you about him, remember?"

No, she hadn't. Maybe she'd told Grandma but not me. "Doesn't ring a bell."

"Lou Miley. He was this grumpy old recluse who lived there. One day, Lou came out of the shack where he lived and found Karson sleeping on an old car seat. Lou brought him a blanket. Karson had been sneaking in and sleeping there for a month by that point. I'm not sure if Lou knew the whole time or what, but he didn't make Karson leave."

It baffled me that an adult wouldn't have called the authorities and rescued those kids. The few times she and Gemma had spoken about the junkyard, they'd made it seem like it was paradise. They'd preferred it to an actual home in the foster care system.

I didn't get it, but I'd stopped trying to make sense of it.

Kat had done what she'd had to do at too young an age to make the best of a shitty situation. She was good at finding the bright side. Whenever we watched a bad movie, she'd spout three things she liked about it during the credits.

Once, we'd run out of coffee in the middle of a blizzard. The roads had been too snowy to traverse so she'd set up a tea station and tried to get me to like tea. I'd sampled every flavor from a variety pack that day, then lied and told her tea wasn't so bad. It was shit compared to coffee, but she'd tried.

"Gemma was the second one to move to the junkyard. Her home was . . ." Kat shook her head. "It was awful. Has she ever talked to you about it?"

"No, and I never asked." In the past six months, I'd gotten to know Gemma fairly well. The two of us worked side by side nearly every day and I couldn't have dreamed up a better partner for Easton, not just because she adored my brother but because she was a damn riot. Feisty and sarcastic, confident and bold, Gemma hadn't been born with the last name Greer, but she would wear it well. You'd never know her childhood had been hell.

"She doesn't tell many people the story," Katherine said.

Kind of like you.

I'd earned Kat's trust in so many other areas. With horses, when I'd taught her to ride. With the stress from work, when she was the one who needed to vent. Hell, she trusted me to cook dinner every Wednesday without backup. So why wouldn't she trust me with her past?

"Anyway," Kat continued, "after Gemma moved to the junkyard, Londyn came next. Actually, Gemma hauled her there after she found Londyn trying to eat a sandwich from a garbage can."

"Did you do that?" My stomach rolled. I hated this for her. "Eat garbage?"

"No, we never ate garbage. There was always food around. We'd have peanut butter and honey sandwiches. The trunk to the Cadillac was a great pantry. But if I never eat another banana, I'll die happy. Same with green beans."

"That's why you don't like Grandma's green bean casserole at Thanksgiving or Christmas." Mom would always send us home with some leftovers but Katherine wouldn't touch it. I'd always thought she was just leaving it for me because it was my favorite holiday side dish.

Kat's face puckered. "That's a no on the green beans. It's a miracle I can stand to eat pizza. Londyn waitressed at a pizza place and she'd bring us back pizza most nights she worked."

"Heaven," I teased.

She laughed. "Even you would have gotten sick of pizza."

"Never."

We didn't get a lot of pizza at the ranch. Delivery to

the boonies wasn't an option, which was probably why I insisted on it whenever we visited a town with a Domino's.

"Okay, keep going." *Please, keep going.* "Tell me more about Aria."

"She and Clara were a year younger than the rest of us. I think they might have come to Montana with us if we would have waited but . . . we had to get out of there."

"Understandable. Were they mad?"

"No, I don't think so. And it was better they stayed where it was safe until they turned eighteen. Karson promised to stay with them at the junkyard until their birthday. I assume he lived in this car until he left."

It made sense now, why the car was supposed to get to California. "Londyn wants Karson to have the Cadillac."

Katherine nodded. "Londyn and Karson dated. They lived in this car together. After she got it restored and left Boston, she wanted him to have it."

"Why didn't she take it to him?"

"That was the plan, but she got a flat tire in West Virginia, fell in love with her mechanic and never made it to California. Instead, she let Gemma take it."

"And Gemma got waylaid by Easton."

"Exactly." Katherine laughed. "This trip was Gemma's idea. Londyn passed the car to Gemma. Gemma passed it to me. And I'll, hopefully, pass it to Aria, who might take it to Karson."

This wasn't just a vacation for Kat. It was a sentimental trip. "Thanks for letting me come along."

She arched an eyebrow over the brim of her new shades. "Did I have a choice?"

"Nope."

She smiled.

"This is cool. The handoff thing. I guess the only difference is that you're coming back home when it's all done."

Kat shifted in her seat and the smile fell from her face. Her fingers flexed around the wheel. She kept her eyes aimed straight ahead and the sudden stiffness in her shoulders made me pause.

She was coming home, right? This wasn't the same type of trip her friends had taken. Kat had a life in Montana. A job. A family. With the mountains and the open range and the clean air, she'd always told me that Montana was where her heart had found home.

She was coming home. That's why she didn't answer. It was a given.

She was coming home.

"Whose idea was it to come to Montana?" I asked.

"Mine." Her smile reappeared. "I thought it sounded like an adventure. I saved up some change to buy a map, then I marked the biggest towns. Every day, I'd walk to a pay phone and call the local newspapers in Bozeman, Billings, Missoula and Great Falls, asking for any new classifieds."

"And they read them to you?"

She nodded. "The receptionists took pity on me. The

paper in Great Falls only did twice so I stopped calling them. After a couple of weeks, I heard about the ad Carol had placed for housekeepers. I called her that day and inquired about it. She told me that if we could get to Montana, there'd be a job waiting. So we waited until I turned eighteen, because I was younger than Londyn and Gemma, then we left. We saved up for bus tickets and . . . you know the rest."

Yes, I knew the rest. There wasn't much I didn't know about Katherine's life since she'd come to Montana. "I'm glad you found that ad."

"Me too."

I twisted to the backseat, where I'd tossed a baseball cap, and pulled it on, trapping the strands of my mostly dry hair. Then I relaxed in my seat.

There were more questions I wanted to ask. Why was she so insistent about not returning to California? Why had she arranged this last-minute trip and not told me about it? But Kat had confided in me more today than she had in years. When I was training a young horse, I didn't push my luck. I wasn't going to with Kat either.

So I flipped Grandma's quarter a couple of times above my lap. "Oregon, here we come."

CHAPTER FOUR

KATHERINE

o.

N *No, Cash.*

No, you may not come on this trip with me.

Why was it so easy to say *no* to Cash in my head but not in person? So much for my trip alone. Damn it. When he'd told me about dumping Dany for me, my resolve to take this solo vacation had disintegrated like wet toilet paper.

Except he hadn't broken it off with her *for* me. *Because* of me. The distinction was essential.

Cash snored in the passenger seat. He'd tipped his hat over his eyes and straight nose. His beard looked soft, like a dog's fur, and I was tempted to sneak a touch.

He grew a beard every November, calling it his winter hide, much like what his horses grew. And like the animals, he'd lose it once the tulips bloomed. Cash would pick a random day to shave and waltz into the kitchen with a grin on his face, proudly displaying that razor-sharp jaw.

I'd miss that annual ritual. I'd miss seeing him every day. But over the last fifty miles, as he'd slept, I'd come to a decision. I couldn't live with Cash. It was time for me to move out.

I'd start with the staff quarters and search for a house of my own.

It would be awkward, returning to the quarters. My time there had been fun, but that had been years ago. The age gap between me and the others was noticeably wider. The younger staff needed a chance to unwind, and having their boss next door was a major buzz kill, but they'd have to deal with it for a while.

There wasn't much of a real estate market in Clear River, but I might find a fixer-upper with projects galore to keep me occupied at night. I'd find something and establish some distance from Cash.

This trip would be our last hurrah. Part of me was glad he'd turned alpha-male brute and insisted on tagging along.

We'd flipped Carol's quarter five times and fate had brought us north and east, over the narrow and quiet Montana highways. There were hours of daylight remaining but as the sun began to lower on the horizon, I wound along a river.

I turned on the radio, scanning for a local channel,

then dropped the volume low, letting the twangy jingle of classic country fill the car.

Cash thought I hated the radio on road trips, probably because that's what I'd told him. Really, I hated the radio when *he* was in the car. He didn't hum along or sing the lyrics. That I could handle, even if it was off-key. No, he had this whistle—this ear-splitting, toothy whistle—that was my equivalent of nails on a chalkboard.

That whistle was nearly as annoying as his tendency to let crumbs pile up around the legs beneath his dining room chair. For days, they'd accumulate until finally I couldn't take it anymore and would vacuum them up.

The thing that had irritated me the most was when Cash had christened me Kat. God, how I'd despised that name in the beginning. Of course, I was the only one. He'd started calling me Kat the year after he'd moved home from college, and every member of the Greer family plus the ranch and resort employees had jumped on the *Kat* hay wagon. I'd stayed quiet, not wanting to alienate the family or my coworkers, despite how the name grated on me. I didn't need constant reminders that I was the short and small one of the bunch. That I was the *runt*.

But then Easton had asked Cash why Kat instead of Kate or Katie. Cash shrugged and told him it was because he admired my claws.

That moment had been another ring around the tree, another moment my love for Cash had grown. I adored the man, piercing whistle and table crumbs included.

The evening air was cool and when I leaned my elbow on the door, the glass of the window was cold against my skin. Covering a yawn with my hand, I kept watch for a sign nestled between the trees, anything to mark an upcoming town. Hopefully one large enough for a motel with two vacancies.

It was exhilarating, not knowing exactly where we were. My entire life, I'd always known my place. I couldn't recall a time when I'd been lost. Trapped, yes, but never lost. Trapped with a mother who'd hated her daughter from the day she was born.

One would think Mom would have screamed *hallelujah* the day I'd left—or had attempted to leave. Instead, she'd slapped me across the face and dragged me to my room, confining me inside for the worst week of my life.

My hand drifted to my cheek. There were still days when I could feel the smack of her palm.

The conversation with Cash must have brought up the memory. I hadn't thought about my mother in months. I shoved her aside, into the box where I kept the past locked away. Cash had rattled the chain around it with his questions earlier.

A sign approached on the road's shoulder. The Idaho border was five miles ahead.

"Hey." Cash shifted in his seat, sitting up. "Sorry, I fell asleep."

"That's okay."

"Where are we?" His deep, husky voice sent a shiver down my spine as he blinked sleep from his eyes.

"We're crossing into Idaho."

He rubbed his jaw. "Want to stop or keep going? I can drive for a while."

"Let's stop." There was no rush. "I want dinner. Maybe we can crash here tonight and start again in the morning."

"Sounds good."

We crossed a long bridge that stretched over the river I'd been driving beside. On the other side, a small town greeted us with welcome signs and the American flag. At the first stop sign, I scanned up and down the streets, searching for a motel.

"Want me to check?" Cash dug his phone from his jeans pocket.

"No. Let's just explore." Eventually we'd have to engage the GPS, but for this first day, I wanted to simply find my way. To embrace the adventure.

"All right." Cash plucked our quarter from the cupholder, positioning it on a knuckle and flicking the edge with his thumbnail. Up it went, end over end, until it smacked in his palm. "Heads."

"Left." I cranked the wheel.

That quarter was lucky. Three blocks down, a neon-orange sign caught my eye with the word *Vacancy* illuminated. Across the street from the Imperial Inn was a restaurant, Harry's Supper Club. The letter board beneath an arrow dotted with light bulbs advertised *Daily Prime Rib Special.*

"Here?" I asked.

"Sold," Cash said. "I'm starving."

"Dinner first." I pulled into the parking lot of Harry's and twisted to grab my purse from the back. The restaurant was dim compared to the bright evening light outside. The décor, rustic and primarily wood, would have fit well at the ranch. But the smell—my God, the smell—made my stomach growl.

Juicy steak and homemade rolls and fluffy potatoes. I was practically drooling by the time the hostess escorted us to a navy booth in the corner. The light hanging over our table gave off a golden glow, enough to reflect glare off the plastic-covered menus. We ordered our drinks and as the waitress described the prime rib special, Cash and I shared the same hungry look.

"Two, please," he told her. "Medium rare. Ranch on the salads. Extra croutons on mine. No tomatoes on hers."

Someday, when—if—I decided to start dating, I hoped the man I chose to sit across from me would take as much notice as Cash so he'd be able to order exactly what I wanted too. It wasn't like I couldn't order myself, but it made me feel special, cherished, that someone knew me well enough to place my order for me.

"We should have made a note of how many miles were on the Cadillac before we started today," Cash said after the waitress delivered our waters. "Would be interesting to know exactly how far we go."

"Oh, I wrote it down in the car."

Cash chuckled. "Always one step ahead of me."

I smiled. "I try."

"So tell me more about the junkyard." He leaned back in the booth, draping one long arm across the back.

He'd worn a long-sleeved Henley today, a shirt I'd bought him two years ago for Christmas because I'd thought the grayish green would bring out the matching flecks in his eyes. The sleeves were pushed up toward his elbows and the muscles on his forearms were tight ropes, strong and defined from years of physical work. The cotton clung to his biceps and stretched across his broad chest. The buttons at the collar were open, revealing a sliver of tan skin and barely a hint of dark hair.

Damn, I'd done good with that shirt. I dropped my eyes to my water, taking a long gulp, hoping the cold liquid would squelch the fire spreading through my veins.

It would be a lot easier to fall out of love with Cash if he weren't so attractive. But how was I supposed to ignore that gorgeous face? How was I supposed to act ambivalent toward that Herculean body and how Cash wielded it with surprising grace? And the way that man looked on a horse, the way his hips glided in a saddle and his bulky thighs clenched—a dull throb bloomed in my core. Even the mental image of him on horseback was intoxicating.

Ignore Cash? *Impossible.* I might as well attempt to drive the Cadillac to the moon.

"Kat."

I blinked, forcing my eyes away from my glass. "Huh?"

"The junkyard. Tell me about it. Or about growing up in California."

I scrunched up my nose. If there was a topic to take my mind off this insane attraction to my best friend, California was the winner. The state itself wasn't to blame. Many loved its temperate weather and abundance of activities and Hollywood flair. But when I thought of California, I thought of my mother.

Cash was tugging on my memory box's chain again.

"Did you decide on a name for that new foal yet?" I asked, hoping to steer the conversation away from my past. It might have worked had any other person sat opposite me.

"Daisy. And I see what you're doing here." Cash's chuckle drifted across the table, the low vibration melting into my bones. "I don't want to talk about home or work. Tell me something I don't know. Pretend it's a date and we're getting to know each other."

A date.

I gulped. This wasn't a date. Yes, we were at a nice restaurant in a secluded booth. The lack of a bustling crowd meant the room was hushed, weaving the illusion of intimacy. But this wasn't a romance.

This wasn't a date.

Except it felt like one. Not that I'd been on many lately. It was hard to go out with one man when you were in love with another.

Was it love? Could it be love when it was so exceptionally unrequited? I'd never been in love before. Maybe this was infatuation. Or a deep, respectful friendship.

Because true love was shared.

My feelings were most definitely not.

"Are you okay?" Cash asked, dropping his forearms to the table as he leaned closer.

No. I wasn't okay. "Just tired," I lied. "It was a long day of driving."

"Tomorrow, it's my turn."

"Okay." I wouldn't argue. Though the Cadillac was a powerful, sleek machine, after nine hours behind the wheel, it had lost some of its shine.

"So tell me more about the junkyard," Cash pressed again.

"You know most of it." Wasn't talking about it in the car enough for one day? Normally, I would have skimped on some of the details that I'd told him earlier, but it seemed important he understand a little more than the basics before we met Aria, if only so he didn't feel left out.

"What about school?" he asked.

"Why do you care?"

"Because this is the one part of your life that I don't know everything about. Indulge me."

No.

It was right there. One easy little word. I didn't have trouble telling Easton no. Or their mom, Liddy. Or JR. Or Jake. The only person I struggled to deny was Carol.

And Cash.

He'd inherited her tenacity and persistence. Coupled with that sexy smile, he was my ultimate weakness.

I caved.

"You already know about school," I said. "I dropped out and earned my GED the year after I moved to the ranch."

"That's right. Mom helped you study."

"Every day at lunch." Liddy would come to the lodge and I'd take a break from cleaning or laundry. We'd sit in the kitchen, eating sandwiches, and she'd help explain any concepts I was struggling with. Not that there were many. Getting my GED had been a piece of cake.

"She told me once that you didn't need her help," Cash said.

"I didn't. But I really liked eating lunch with her every day."

Liddy had been the mother who'd shown me how horrendous my own had been. Maybe when I moved out of Cash's place, she'd help me decorate. She could teach me how to cultivate a garden. Liddy would understand my need for some space, right?

"She liked eating lunch with you too. Mom always said she fell in love with you over that GED book."

"Same here," I whispered. "I owe her a lot. Carol too. All of you."

"You don't owe us anything, Kat. You're family."

Family. *The sister.* It had been harder and harder not to feel bitter lately. Being part of the Greer family, even unofficially, was a dream. For a woman who had no family, belonging to one was all I'd ever wanted. So why couldn't I get over my own selfish crush, put this attraction aside and just be *family?*

I looked up and my heart—my sadistic heart—skipped. *That's why.*

Cash's face was shadowed by the dim light. His hair was a mess from being in a hat all day. He'd taken it off when we'd sat down because he wouldn't wear it at the dinner table. It intensified his sparkling gaze. It defined that bearded jaw and accentuated the soft pout of his lower lip. He was mysterious and sexy and utterly mouthwatering.

Screw you, heart.

I don't love Cash.

From now until the end of this trip, I'd tell myself constantly.

I don't love Cash.

"Where did you work? When you lived at the junkyard?" he asked.

I really didn't feel like delving into the past once more, but the alternative wasn't an option. I couldn't sit here

65

across from Cash with his unassuming smolder and pretend the sight of him wasn't making me wet.

Talking was the lesser of two evils. "I worked at a car wash. Karson worked there too. The owner was kind of a jerk but he paid in cash and didn't ask questions."

When I'd filled out the application, I'd put the junk-yard's address as my own. Gemma had been listed as my guardian, Londyn a personal reference. Both had been listed with bogus phone numbers. If the owner had known, he hadn't cared. He'd hired me on the spot.

"Is that how you met Karson? At the car wash?"

"Um, sort of." This was why I didn't want to open that box. One question led to another, then another, and I wouldn't lie to Cash.

"Sort of?"

I sighed. "Yes, I met Karson at the car wash, but not as a coworker. I was on the sidewalk, begging for money." It felt as pathetic to admit years later as it had at the time.

The easy look on Cash's face disappeared as a crease formed between his eyebrows. "What?"

I lifted a shoulder. "I was broke."

"Kat—"

"Don't worry. It was just an experiment. That was the first and last time," I said, cutting him off before he could ask questions. Maybe if I steered this conversation in the right direction, we could just avoid anything that would lead to a conversation about the pre-junkyard days.

Not even Carol or Liddy knew that whole story.

"Did you text your dad? Will he check on the house and water my plants while we're gone?" I asked.

"Nice try, sweetheart." Cash shook his head.

Sweetheart. As if Kat weren't enough of a nickname. Why had he given me a pet name too? It was so endearing and affectionate and . . . sexless. Like I was an eight-year-old girl.

"There's nothing more to explain. I didn't have a penny to my name and I really wanted some money to buy a new pair of shoes."

"Why'd you need the shoes?"

"Does it matter?"

"Kat."

"Cash."

His gaze drilled into mine, and that stare, combined with the stubborn set of his jaw, brooked no argument. His expression mimicked Easton's more scrutinizing gaze. "Why did you need the shoes?"

"Because the only pair that fit were flip-flops," I blurted. "And I was days away from turning sixteen so I could apply for a real job. I'd already talked to the manager at a fast-food place, but she told me I needed closed-toe shoes for work."

It had always struck me as ironic that I couldn't get a job to earn the money to buy the shoes without the shoes themselves. Asking my mother for money had been out of the question since I'd been lucky to have the flip-flops in the first place.

"I sat on a street corner with a cardboard sign and a chipped, green plastic cup that I'd taken from my house. And I earned seven dollars and ten cents."

Cash sat perfectly still. Even his chest was frozen, like he'd forgotten how to breathe. But his eyes said everything he wasn't going to voice.

"Please, don't look at me like that." I'd worked so hard to prove myself. To be the strong, capable woman in charge of an award-winning Montana resort.

Cash cleared his throat. "Sorry."

"You can't pity that girl, because she's me. And without her, I wouldn't be sitting across from you right now."

"I don't pity you, Kat." His expression gentled and he blew out a deep breath. "I don't like to think of you living like that. Begging for money. It hurts."

And that was why loving Cash Greer was so damn easy. My pain was his pain. Part of the reason I didn't want him to know my story was because then it would hurt us both.

"I didn't have to beg for long," I said. "I had been sitting there for about three hours, hot and embarrassed and miserable, when Karson came over and introduced himself. He gave me twenty dollars and offered me a place to stay."

The kid living in the junkyard had given me more than money. He'd given me hope.

"Wait." Cash's face hardened. "Did he proposition you? Because you talk like Karson is this good guy but—"

"No." I laughed, realizing how it must have sounded. "Nothing like that. If it was any other person than Karson, I would have run away screaming. But he *is* a good guy. He sat down beside me. Told me that he'd run away from home and where he was living. And he told me about Gemma and Londyn."

"He could have been lying," Cash said.

"But he wasn't. I went with him to the junkyard that day to scope it out." I'd walked with Karson across town to the junkyard, curious and desperate. I'd returned home determined. The plan I'd concocted that day hadn't exactly turned out as I'd expected, but eventually, I'd found my way back. To Karson. To Gemma. To Londyn. To the start of a new life.

"Here you go." The waitress arrived at the edge of our table, carrying two overloaded platters. She slid them in front of us, refilled our waters, then left us alone with our food.

Dinner halted our conversation as we tore into the meal. I, for one, was grateful for the reprieve. We ate mostly in silence, devouring the meal, and paid the check —Cash insisted because I'd driven all day. He never let me pay for a meal out, always finding an excuse to treat me— cleaning the house, washing his towels. He wouldn't let me pay at a restaurant but didn't argue about splitting the grocery bill. Men made no sense.

But after a decade of arguing, with not only him but all the Greer men, who refused to let a woman cover the dinner bill, I'd admitted defeat. I believed in gender equality and empowering women, but I also recognized it was something Cash needed. It was his way to show gratitude.

"Thanks for dinner," I said as we climbed into the Cadillac.

"Welcome. Thanks for letting me tag along."

"Ha," I deadpanned. "Did I have a choice?"

"Nope." He grinned, reached across the cab and flicked the tip of my nose.

I swatted him away, smiling as we drove across the street to the motel.

The rooms at the Imperial Inn were all outward facing. The building was L shaped, with an office at one end that smelled like fresh coffee and vanilla air freshener. After the clerk handed over the keys to two neighboring rooms, Cash and I reparked the Cadillac closer to where we'd be staying and he hauled my suitcase inside.

"This is nice," I said, tossing my purse on the fluffy, floral bedspread. The room was modest but clean. It wasn't the Greer Resort, but nothing was.

"Do me a favor," Cash said, setting my leather suitcase beside the closet. "Don't open the door unless it's me. I've never liked places where the doors open to the outside."

"No problem." I'd seen enough horror movies and thrillers to fear the knock on the motel room door after dark. My lock would remain deadbolted until sunrise. "What time do you want to leave in the morning?"

"Seven?"

"Okay." I nodded. "Have a good night."

"You too." He crossed the room and bent low, wrapping me in a hug.

I slid my hands around his waist, burrowing into his strong shoulder and taking one long heartbeat to savor his strength. To soak up his spicy cologne and heady, masculine scent. I dragged it through my nose, holding it in.

His arms drew me closer.

I squeezed my eyes shut, pretending for a split second this was real. That this embrace was more than a friend wishing another friend good night. Then before I was ready, he was gone.

The heat from his chest disappeared, replaced by the cool night air, as he took a too-long step away.

Cash's forehead furrowed as he stared down at me, a look of shock marring his handsome face.

Oh my God, I'd sniffed him. I'd sniffed him and he'd heard and now things were weird. *Shit*. And I'd been holding on to him so tight. I'd been clinging to him. *Clinging*. What did I do? What did I say? My brain was scrambling for any way to downplay that hug, but before I could make up some lame excuse about feeling lonely or tired, Cash patted the top of my head and strode out of the room, the door swinging closed behind him.

I waited, listening to his bootsteps, as he walked down

the sidewalk to his room. The door opened and shut, echoing through our adjoining wall. Then it was silent, the insulation between our rooms preventing me from hearing anything else.

I blew out the breath I'd been holding. Mortification flamed across my cheeks.

Did he know? Had that hug just given me away? There was a reason I kept a safe physical distance from Cash. Two feet at minimum. Because apparently my body couldn't be trusted.

I groaned, collapsing onto the end of the bed and burying my face in my hands.

Cash had patted my head.

I'd hugged him, sniffed him, and he'd patted my head.

What the fuck was wrong with me? Why was I doing this to myself? Why couldn't I just shut it off?

I don't love Cash.

I don't love Cash.

I don't—

A sob came out of nowhere and escaped my lips. I slapped a hand over my mouth in case there was another. This roller coaster was killing me. We were friends one minute, talking and eating and laughing, then the next I just wanted him to hold me. To say good night with a kiss instead of a childish pat on the damn head.

Why was letting him go so hard?

Why couldn't he love me back?

CHAPTER FIVE

CASH

"Cash," Kat snapped as the tires buzzed on the rumble strip.

I jerked my gaze up and righted the car before drifting into the other lane. Thankfully it was empty.

Fuck. What was with me today?

"What's with you today?" she asked.

Of course she'd snatch the words from my head. The two of us had been friends for so long, it wasn't uncommon to finish each other's sentences.

"Sorry," I muttered. "Just, uh, lost in thought."

Katherine hummed and returned her gaze to the passenger window, staring out over the green fields that rolled beyond. Her attention had been fixed on the landscape all morning, which was probably why she hadn't noticed that the reason I'd been bouncing between the white line of the shoulder and yellow center divide for the past twenty miles was because my eyes hadn't exactly been on the road.

They'd been on her.

I ran a hand over my jaw, then gave it a smack, wishing I could knock some sense into my head. Since I hadn't shaved my beard yet, maybe it would cover some of the confusion on my face.

Something was not right. Things felt . . . weird. With Kat. And I couldn't put my finger on why.

Last night, we'd had a normal dinner. At least, it should have been normal. Just two friends sitting across from one another, talking. And she'd confided in me. Finally, Kat had trusted me with details from her past.

Was that why dinner had felt so . . . intimate? Maybe it was just the setting, but damn, it had felt like a date. I'd teased her about thinking of it like one but hadn't expected to actually fall for it myself. And not just a date.

A good date.

The best date.

I shook my head and gripped the steering wheel harder. *Eyes on the road. Do not look at her knees.*

They were just knees, like the shoulder I'd been glancing at a minute ago was just a shoulder. It was only bare skin, smooth and creamy. Flawless except for the one freckle that dotted the apex of her arm and the other that peeked out from the hem of her denim shorts.

When had Kat gotten freckles? Why was I noticing today?

I reached for the console and cranked up the air conditioning. Maybe if it was colder she'd cover those knees and shoulders and skin with something. Because Kat hated to be cold and if I dropped it low enough in here, she'd produce the sweater that was no doubt hiding in that suitcase she called a purse.

When had Kat begun showing so much skin? Normally she wore jeans and long sleeves, her shirts always embroidered with the resort's logo. Even on weekend workdays, she wore a T-shirt and jeans. Was that even a tank top? With its lace trim and satin sheen, it looked more like lingerie.

The temperature had spiked today and the sun was beating down on us since she'd asked to drive with the top down for a while.

"Why did you turn the air on?" she asked, looking above us to the open air.

"I'm hot." *Desperate.* What would it take for her to put on a goddamn sweater? "Are you wearing sunscreen?"

"Uh, no." She gave me a sideways glance. "Why?"

"You're going to get burned." *Get the sweater, Kat. You know you want to.*

"I'll be fine. At the next gas station, I'll grab a bottle for us."

Us. Why did that word sound so serious? It wasn't the intimate kind of us. There was no us. Not in the couple sense of the word. Did I want there to be an us?

Yes.

That lightning-fast internal response nearly had me slamming on the brakes, turning this car around and going back to Montana, where the world was normal.

Kat was my friend. My best friend. Roommate. Coworker. Pseudo sibling. There were days when I'd trade Easton for her permanently. Okay, any day. There were plenty of ways to label our relationship and *us* was not one.

I could not—would not—tear down the boundaries that nearly a decade and firm family reminders had put in place.

Yes, Kat was a beautiful woman. But like I'd told myself at the beginning, after my family had practically adopted her, Kat was off-limits. A single prime-rib dinner and a trip to Oregon weren't going to change that.

I was blaming Harry's Supper Club and the Imperial Inn. That goddamn hotel. Tonight, we were sure as fuck staying somewhere nicer. A hotel with working alarm clocks and decent towels. Big towels. Towel sheets. The scraps they'd justified in the Imperial were a goddamn joke.

Because maybe if I hadn't witnessed Kat clutching a scrap of terry cloth to her naked, dripping-wet body this morning, I wouldn't be so spellbound by her knees. It would be easier for me to remember that she was off-fuck-ing-limits.

Fuck you, towels.

I'd woken up this morning at my normal time, around

five thirty. I'd showered and done my best to shake off the non-date dinner. Then I'd dressed, packed my bag and gone to Katherine's room.

I'd knocked once and waited. Then twice. After the third time with no answer, I'd been ready to kick the door in when her footsteps had sounded, running for the deadbolt and chain.

Kat had flung the door open and my mouth had gone desert dry.

The image was printed on my mind like a brand on a steer's hide, burned there forever.

Her hair had been dripping wet, the dark strands depositing glistening drops on her skin. They'd run over her shoulders and down the line of her neck and collarbone. They'd raced over the swells of her breasts, disappearing into the towel.

Her face had been clean and her cheeks flushed, like she'd raced through the end of her shower to answer the door.

She'd rambled something about an alarm clock and her phone not being charged and sleeping late. Her words had been a jumble, delivered so fast they hadn't penetrated my haze, but I could recall with vivid clarity how her lips had moved, soft and pink and ripe. The hand not clutching the towel had flailed in the air as she'd spoken, the movement causing the terry cloth on her left breast to slip and a hint of areola to show. The hem of that towel had barely covered the supple cheeks of her ass as she'd dashed toward the closet to pull out some clothes, only to disappear into the bathroom to get dressed.

I'd forced myself to close her hotel room door, her on the inside, me on the outside, and suck in some damn air as I'd tried to get my hard-on under control.

I'd gotten hard for Kat. My Kat. Katherine Gates, my incredibly sexy, incredibly off-limits best friend.

Kat would come along with me and some buddies whenever I took the family boat to the lake on rare summer weekends off. I'd threatened many friends with death by drowning because of the way they'd ogled her in a bikini.

I'd seen her in less than that towel. I'd seen her countless times after a shower. Granted, normally she wore the lavender puff monstrosity of a robe that my mother had bought her for Christmas a few years ago. It covered her from neck to calf but it was still after-shower attire.

But damn that towel.

I'd wanted to strip it from her body and taste her lips, discover for myself if they were as sweet and pure and clean as the water droplets clinging to her skin.

This was crazy. Fuck, I was losing my mind.

And I was hard again.

Son of a bitch.

"Do you want me to drive?" she asked, shifting in the seat. She tucked one ankle under the opposite knee and the position meant there was a lot of long, lean thigh in my periphery.

My eyes zeroed in on the dotted yellow line that broke the asphalt into halves. I refused to look at her leg. "No."

"Okay." She plucked the quarter out of the metal ashtray, where we'd stashed it.

Ahead, a sign indicated we were about ten miles away from the next town and the interstate. Idaho was long gone, apparently along with my self-control. We were in Washington, headed south.

"Let's flip to see if we go straight or turn."

" 'Kay." I nodded. "Heads, we keep south. Tails, we go east or west. We'll flip again to decide."

The coin turned end over end above her lap and landed with a light thud in her palm. She slapped it on the back of her opposite hand. "Tails."

That meant we'd be getting on the interstate. East would take us toward Montana. Part of me wished for east, longing for the normalcy of home. But I knew Kat. She wasn't going to be satisfied until the Cadillac was delivered, which meant whether I liked it or not, we were headed to Oregon.

Heads. Come on, heads.

She repeated the flip. "Heads."

"West," I breathed.

At least fate was sympathetic to my pain. If the coin flips continued to go in my favor, we'd keep this up. Maybe this attraction was a temporary glitch and tomorrow morning I'd feel differently. But if not, the second that quarter began to work against me, I was tossing it out the window and punching Heron Beach into the GPS.

"Want to stop?" I asked as we neared a gas station beside the interstate's onramp.

"Yes, please."

I nodded and eased off the road, deciding to fill up too and parking beside the pump.

"Are you coming in?" Kat hopped out and slid her sunglasses into her hair. It blew in the breeze and as a few wisps tickled her forehead, she lifted an arm to brush them away.

That move wasn't anything I hadn't seen a hundred times, but I sat in the driver's seat, transfixed. She'd curled her hair again, for the second day in a row. It was as long as it had ever been, the glossy locks tumbling over the spaghetti straps of her dainty top.

"Cash."

I blinked. *Fuck. My. Life.* "Yeah, I'll be in after I gas up."

"Okay." Her long legs were impossible to ignore as she crossed the parking lot to the convenience store. I mean, they weren't long. Not at all. I could pick her up with one arm and toss her over my shoulder, she was that small. But damn they looked long. Miles of smooth, tight skin leading down from an ass that my cock wanted to kiss.

I dropped my eyes to my zipper and the bulge forming beneath. "Fuck you."

This couldn't be happening. I couldn't have the hots for Kat. She'd laugh in my damn face.

We were friends.

We'd been friends for over a decade.

I shoved my door open and went about getting gas, taking a few moments to get myself in check. It wasn't like these thoughts were completely foreign. It wasn't like today was the first time I'd noticed that Katherine Gates was a gorgeous woman.

But today, it was like my body had finally had enough of my mind games.

After twelve years, denial's ironclad grip was beginning to falter, and without my family around, there was no constant reminder that I was expected to behave a certain way where Kat was concerned. That they'd kill me if I broke her heart.

Yes, Kat and I had spent plenty of time together at home without my body getting overheated. But it was my grandparents' former house.

Last night, she'd confided in me. She'd trusted me. And how was I repaying her? By sporting a goddamn chubby all day and gawking at her body.

I was such a fucking asshole.

The nozzle on the gas pump popped and I returned it to its cradle, closing the cap on the Cadillac's tank before stuffing the keys in my pocket and walking into the store.

Katherine snared my attention instantly. She was standing in the candy aisle, her eyebrows furrowed. She was probably trying to decide between a salted nut roll or chocolate bar. Sure enough, I rounded the corner and she held one in one hand and the other in the opposite.

"Get both."

She looked at me and frowned. "You always say that."

I chuckled and walked closer, bending in front of her to pick up my own salted nut roll. On the way up, I miscalculated, moving too close. My arm brushed against hers and Kat's peach scent drew me in. I hovered, unable to step away.

Her blue eyes lifted to mine and she held my gaze. God, she was close. So damn close. My fingers itched to run up the bare skin of her arm and see if it was as velvety smooth as the fruit she smelled like.

When my gaze dropped to her lips, she gasped.

Christ. I took one long step back, then tossed her my nut roll. What was wrong with me? "I'm, uh . . . gonna use the restroom."

"Okay." She put the chocolate bar back and pointed to the row of coolers along the far wall, not looking at me. "What do you want to drink?"

"Water."

She bolted away so fast her flip-flops nearly slipped on the glossy linoleum surface.

Hell. Now I'd made her uncomfortable.

I marched to the bathroom and splashed a handful of cold water on my face. "Get your shit together, Greer."

The smell of industrial cleaner and a urinal cake

chased Kat's scent from my nose but as soon as we were back in the car, it would be waiting. It was how our house smelled, sweet and fresh. It was not a new smell, yet today, there was a heady, alluring undertone. I'd noticed it last night in the hotel room when she'd hugged me good night.

When she'd come into my arms so easily that for a moment, I'd forgotten I had to let her go.

I used the bathroom, my mood growing more and more irritable with every passing second. When I stalked out of the men's room, Kat was visible through the store's plate glass window, standing beside the Cadillac, her head bent and her fingers flying over the screen of her phone. I walked to the candy aisle, grabbing the chocolate bar she hadn't bought and a pack of gum, delaying my return to the car for just another minute.

This trip was supposed to be fun. Yesterday had been fun, driving wherever the quarter directed. Hearing stories about her past from her own lips. Sharing a good dinner and her company.

Dany's jealousy hadn't been that off base, had it? Last night had stirred emotions that I hadn't wanted to acknowledge—lust, for one.

Well, lust could fuck right off. I wasn't going to sabotage my friendship with Kat just because my cock was going through a dry spell.

I paid the clerk for Kat's chocolate, then squared my shoulders and stalked outside. My steps slowed as I approached and caught the scowl on her face. "What's wrong?"

"Carol told my entire staff not to email me. Which is ironic because Annabeth just emailed me to tell me they aren't allowed to email me."

I chuckled. "Sounds like Grandma."

"Grrr." Kat tossed a hand in the air. "I'm on vacation. I'm not dead."

"She's just trying to help."

"But it's stressing me out. I love my job."

"I know."

"I want to do my job."

"And you can." I stepped closer and put a hand on her shoulder. How many times had I done this? How many times had I touched her? Hundreds. Thousands. Yet like last night when I'd given her a hug, suddenly everything felt differently. I yanked my hand away, the heat from her skin too hot and electric.

She looked at me, then her eyes dropped to the place where I'd touched her. They alternated back and forth, like she was checking to make sure I hadn't wiped a booger on her or something. Then her gaze went to the ground and her shoulders slumped.

"Here." I handed her the chocolate.

"What's this for?"

I shrugged. "Just because."

She lifted her lashes and gave me a sad smile.

"Thanks. Maybe a few hundred empty calories will make me feel better."

"Grandma just wants you to take a vacation. A real vacation. Let her handle whatever happens at home."

"What if there's a crisis?"

"She'll call. Trust me. No news is good news."

"Fine," she muttered. "I feel like I got kicked out."

"No one would ever dream of kicking you out."

She sighed. "I'll take the next shift driving."

I dug the keys from my pocket and handed them over. We'd left the doors unlocked because the top was down, so I gave her some space to walk past me and around the hood before climbing in the passenger seat.

It should have been better riding shotgun, because my gaze could wander, but as we headed west on the interstate, it constantly seemed to drift toward her, like a magnet to steel. My foot bounced on the floor. My hand tapped on my knee.

Kat was stunning behind the wheel, the sun lighting her face and those floating tendrils of hair brushing her shoulders. She'd be even prettier with a smile.

"Tell me more about Aria," I said, hoping to take Kat's mind off work and mine off Kat. "How'd she come to live in the junkyard?"

"Because of Londyn," she said. "They'd lived in the same trailer park. Aria and Clara were living with their uncle. Their parents died in a car accident and the uncle was the only living relative so he got custody. I never saw the guy or met him, but Londyn knew him from their neighborhood. Gemma saw him once when she snuck to their trailer with Aria to steal Clara's bike. I guess he was a major creep. Gemma said he had these beady eyes that made you want to take a shower."

"Did he do something to Aria and Clara?"

"I don't know. It was a no-go subject. They knew that Londyn had run away from her druggie parents and started asking around, trying to find out where she'd gone. They walked into the junkyard one day, holding hands, and that was it. They lived with us." A smile tugged at the corner of her mouth. "They each had these huge back-packs stuffed so tight that when they unzipped them, everything inside just exploded. Clothes. Food. Money. Medicine. They were far more prepared to live there than any of the rest of us had been."

"Londyn and Karson had this Caddy. Gemma and you were in the tent. Where did Aria and Clara stay?"

"In a delivery van. They were smart. They picked a place off the ground and with fewer holes so they didn't have to deal with the mice."

My stomach knotted, like it had yesterday, not wanting to think about Kat sleeping with vermin. "Was it really better than home?"

"Yes." No hesitation.

"What about foster care?"

She shook her head. "That junkyard was my only option."

"And your parents—"

"Should we flip again?" She was already taking out the quarter, balancing the wheel with her knee as she tossed the coin.

At the next exit, Kat got off the interstate and turned on the radio. The music blared, and with the wind whipping over us, it would be impossible to talk.

Conversation over.

She drove with her gaze fixed on the road, never wavering. Never offering another opening to a new topic, certainly not about life before the Greer Ranch and Mountain Resort.

I should have thanked her because instead of thinking about the bare skin of Kat's legs or the slender line of her neck or the graceful drape of her wrist over the steering wheel, I spent the next few hours wondering why my best friend was so hell-bent on keeping secrets.

Maybe she kept hers for the same reason I kept mine.

Because the truth would drive us apart.

CHAPTER SIX

KATHERINE

"Want to flip or . . ." *Please say no. Please say no.* "When are you supposed to meet Aria?" Cash asked.

"There's no schedule. She doesn't even know I'm coming, but I think sooner rather than later."

"Then let's get into Oregon today."

Thank God. I dropped the quarter onto the leather seat, not caring if it got wedged in a crack and disappeared into the Cadillac for life. Then I put the car in drive and pulled away from the motel where we'd stayed last night.

This trip was the worst idea I'd had in years. Actually, it had been Gemma's idea, so I was placing the blame at her feet.

I wanted to get to Heron Beach, give this car to Aria and hop on the nearest plane to Montana. Assuming she'd take the car. Oh God, what if she didn't take the car? What if I had to endure a return trip with Cash?

I sent up a silent prayer that Aria would buy into this whole Cadillac handoff thing because there was no way I'd go to California and I didn't know if I could survive another awkward and tense day with Cash.

So much for a last hurrah.

How had it come to this? How had two people who could finish each other's sentences have so little to say? Never in a million years would I have expected this road trip to be so miserable. I mean, I'd expected it to be hard because I secretly loved him. But no harder than any regular day.

It was my fault. He knew. That first night, Cash must have realized my feelings for him weren't entirely platonic.

Me and my sniffing and lingering hugs. I'd stared too much over dinner at the supper club. I'd been too happy that he'd dumped Dany.

He knew.

Yesterday, he'd barely made eye contact, and when he had, there had been restraint in his gaze, like he was consciously weighing every move. He'd put his hand on my shoulder, realized he'd touched me, probably feared I'd take that gesture to heart, and snatched his hand away so fast he could have dislocated a shoulder.

I'd wanted to crawl under the front tire and let him run me over.

And he wasn't the only one measuring his words. I

was terrified to speak in case he'd see just how deep this crush of mine ran.

This had to end. If we drove straight through today, we could get to the coast. We'd be one step closer to calling this trip a bust and going home.

The radio was on low and it crackled with static so I scanned for a new channel. The Cadillac had satellite radio and Bluetooth for my phone, but having to change stations every hundred miles was at least something to do. A twenty-second pardon from the stifling silence.

Cash recognized the song. Damn. I braced, waiting and . . .

The absentminded, piercing whistle hissed from between his teeth. I'd stopped hiding my cringe.

Not that he'd noticed. Cash was stoically staring down the road.

"How far is it to Heron Beach?" I asked.

Cash entered it into his phone's GPS. "About ten hours."

Stupid quarter. Yesterday, the coin had led us backward. We'd gone south, but much too far east, exactly the opposite direction of where we'd needed to head. The universe was conspiring against me.

We were in Idaho again, having recrossed over from Washington. Last night, we'd stopped before dinner and checked into a hotel on the outskirts of Boise. Rather than force us together for an uncomfortable meal, I'd told Cash I was tired from a long day of driving. We'd picked up sandwiches and eaten alone in our respective rooms.

I'd tried calling Gemma but she hadn't answered. Neither had Liddy or Carol. So I'd found a movie on TV and gone to bed early.

Why had I thought this trip would be more exciting? Sure, the countryside was pretty. There'd been one stretch of highway that had been so shrouded by trees, it was like we'd driven through a leafy, green tunnel. But besides the occasional gas station break, when we loaded up on sugar and junk food, the repetitive miles had begun to take their toll.

"How was your night?" Cash asked. His sunglasses were on, shielding his eyes.

"Fine. Yours?"

He lifted a shoulder. "Fine. Watched a game. Crashed early."

What game? Who won? Did you sleep okay? All questions I'd have normally asked before I'd made things weird. Now I was worried that if he made me laugh, if he made me smile, the wall would crack and he'd see the truth shining through.

I don't love Cash.

Even I wasn't buying my own lies.

"I've been thinking," I said, taking a deep breath. "When we get home, I'm going to start looking for my own place."

"What?" Cash shifted and slid his sunglasses into his

dark hair. His hazel eyes were so colorful this morning, honey swirled with chocolate and sage. Even with the Cadillac's top up, sunlight bounced off the golden flecks.

I kept my eyes on the road and my hands glued to the wheel. There was no way I'd get through this if I was looking at those eyes. "You need your own space. So do I. The roommate thing worked for a while but it doesn't really make sense. We're adults. We can live alone."

"Is this about Dany?"

"No." Partly. When he did find a woman who'd come to his bed, I didn't want to be on the other side of the house.

Cash put his sunglasses on and his bearded jaw ticked as he stared forward. Mile after mile. Minute after minute. His lack of response made my heart sink, beat after beat. Didn't he care? Couldn't he pretend or slightly object or act like he'd enjoyed having me as a roommate for the past five years?

Finally, he said, "Okay."

Okay. Ouch. His rejection was worse than the time my mother had taken a pinch of my skin between her fingers and twisted it so hard that I'd dropped to my knees and vomited. Then she'd made me clean up my mess.

I fought the urge to cry by biting the inside of my cheek. It was a trick I'd learned early on in life. If I concentrated on my teeth, on how my flesh felt pinched tight between the molars, the tears would disappear.

Crying wouldn't get me anywhere. If I cried, Cash

would take pity on me and pity was far worse than any form of heartache.

This was only a change. A shift in—hopefully—the right direction. Some space from Cash and we'd find a normal routine again. We'd go back to being friends. He'd start dating. Maybe I would too. Though the idea of any other man held no appeal but . . . someday.

I wanted a family. My *own* family. Kids who'd run around on the ranch through the green grass in spring and pick wildflowers from the meadows. A dog who'd trail behind them, keeping watch. A husband who'd let me curl into his lap on cold winter afternoons and hold me while the snow fell.

That man wasn't Cash. The sooner I stopped picturing his face in that dream, the sooner I could open my mind and heart to finding love.

"How long?" Cash asked.

"How long, what?" I glanced at him, then back at the road.

"How long have you been planning on moving out? Would you have told me?"

I frowned. "Of course I would have told you."

"Like you told me about taking this trip."

Score one, Cash. "Well, I'm telling you now."

He crossed his arms, stared out the window. "Just like Kat. Keeping the world at arm's length."

"Excuse me?"

"You don't trust any of us. You are part of our family, but there's no trust."

I shook my head. "What are you talking about? Where is this coming from?"

"How long have we known one another? You've never told me about Aria or Clara or Karson or Lou until this trip. Until I peppered you with questions and there wasn't any place for you to go and avoid them."

I sucked in a calming breath. Cash was just lashing out. I'd wanted him to be upset that I was moving out. Well, he was upset. He wasn't wrong. The past was a topic I avoided at all costs, but he also wasn't being fair. He had no idea what I'd undergone, and if I wanted to keep it locked away, that was my choice. "It's not something I like to talk about."

"That's my point."

My knuckles were nearly as white as the steering wheel. "I told you about the junkyard a long, long time ago."

"No, you told Grandma and Mom. Not the same."

Why would I want to tell him about the ugliest times in my life? Why would I want the man I'd been crushing on for years to see my dirty pieces? I'd been clinging to the hope that he'd see me as a sexy, appealing, available woman. Not a pathetic *runt* who'd once been given a stick of deodorant by Mr. Kline, her ninth-grade gym teacher, because she'd smelled and hadn't been able to afford any herself.

Maybe the reason I'd opened up on this trip was because I'd finally given up hope. Cash wouldn't see me as anything more than a friend, a sister, so why hide the truth?

"Can you blame me?" I asked. "Why would I want to talk about it?"

"Because we're *supposed* to be friends. We're supposed to confide in each other."

"We *are* friends."

Cash scoffed. "Then act like it, Katherine. Talk to me."

"I am talking to you!" I threw up a hand. "I'm telling you right now that I want to move out. I need some space."

"From me."

"No." *Yes.* "I just . . . need a change."

"Okay."

There was that word again, laced with sarcasm and disdain. I'd missed the nasty undertones the first time.

The silence returned. The radio was cutting in and out, but I didn't bother changing the channel. My molars ground together. Cash's nostrils flared.

What the hell did he have to be mad about? We were in our thirties. Wouldn't he want a place to himself? Why keep a roommate when he didn't need the financial support? And how dare he tell me that I didn't confide in him.

"You're one to talk about not confiding."

"What?" He shot me a glare. "You know everything there is to know about me."

"Do I? Then let's talk about the ranch."

"What about the ranch?"

"How do you really feel about the expansion?"

It had been Easton's idea to create a state-of-the-art horse breeding and training facility. He'd bought the land for the expansion to the ranch, all the while planning on having Cash run it, but he'd never asked. He'd done it without consulting Cash, or anyone, first.

Cash was fairly easygoing. It took a lot to fluster him, but he was a proud man. He was a leader in his own right. And no one had asked if he even *wanted* to run the training facility. They just assumed that since he loved horses, since he had a gift with the animals, he'd follow suit.

"I'm excited for it." Cash shrugged. "It'll be great once we get it going. I'll get to spend more time with the horses."

"That's not what I'm asking. How do you feel about how it all came about?"

"You mean that East bought property without telling any of us?"

"Yes."

"It's fine." Another shrug. "You know how it is with Dad and Granddad. They aren't great at letting go. This was Easton's power play. He wants to make his mark."

He'd badgered me for not sharing my feelings, but he was doing the same. "But what about you?"

"What about me?"

"Easton should have talked to you. He should have told you what he was planning."

"Maybe."

My temper flared. "Maybe? Yes. He should have talked to you."

"Okay, fine. He should have talked to me. But he didn't."

"Doesn't that make you angry?"

"What do you want me to do about it, Kat? Get into it with Easton? He's already fighting Dad and Granddad on the management stuff. I'm trying to tread lightly and just get the goddamn project done. Why does it matter when at the end of the day, I want to work with horses? This will make that happen."

"But—"

"There's no but. Yes, Easton of all people should know what it's like to feel excluded. To be talked over and brushed aside. But I've known my entire life what it feels like to be in second place. I'm the second son. Causing a fight about it isn't going to change that fact."

It wasn't fair. Cash shouldn't be talked around. He shouldn't be ignored. Didn't he realize how talented he was? How smart?

Why was I angrier about this than he was? Maybe this wasn't an issue for him. Maybe I'd misread the situation.

Or maybe I was picking a fight because moving out when we got home would be a lot easier if I was pissed at

Cash first. If I was going to make him mad, I might as well go all in.

"Why do you let people decide how your life is going to go?" I regretted the question immediately.

Cash turned to stone.

My stomach plummeted. Now who wasn't being fair? Cash didn't let people dictate his life, but his family was packed full of strong personalities. They didn't walk over him per se. He just didn't battle.

I couldn't remember a time when Cash argued with his parents or grandparents or Easton. Which was a good thing, except in a family where a Friday dinner wasn't a Friday dinner without some sort of bickering. It had always struck me as off that Cash was rarely in the fray.

He sat motionless and unspeaking, his expression passive. The tension was so thick, his soundless rage so consuming, my own guilt so heavy, that I struggled to breathe.

One hour bled into two. Five to six.

As we drove out of Idaho and into Oregon, I spent the passing miles attempting not to cry. I'd bitten the inside of my cheeks so hard I'd drawn blood.

The farmland around us was a brilliant kelly green. Fences broke up fields. Snowcapped peaks rose tall above the sweeping valleys in the distance. It was a beautiful day outside, bright and clear. But the storm brewing inside the car was as black as midnight.

Hour after hour, regret ate a hole through me like acid

through an apple. I wanted to apologize, to make this right, but Cash was too furious to listen. And I was too afraid that if I opened my mouth, too much truth would escape.

Maybe he suspected I had feelings for him, but I'd spent many, many years with my secrets guarded. I wouldn't confess my feelings now.

We had to stop. I had to get out of this car.

A sign along the road marked eight miles to the next town. The gas pump, restaurant and hotel icons indicated it offered services and lodging. We'd made considerable progress today and Heron Beach was only hours away. We'd be there before nightfall if I kept driving.

But I was so weary, so desperate to stop, that I pulled off the highway at the first hotel.

"You don't want to keep going?" Cash asked as I parked.

"Not tonight." My voice was hoarse as I tried to speak past the choking lump in my throat. "I'd rather get there fresh tomorrow to find Aria. Is that okay?"

"It's your trip." He opened his door and stepped out, going to the trunk.

I sucked in a deep breath. Fifteen minutes. I only had to make it fifteen minutes, then I'd be in my room and I could cry alone.

After popping the trunk, I collected my things from the car and climbed out, locking the doors as Cash carried my suitcase in one hand, his duffel in the other, into the lobby.

"Good evening," the clerk greeted, a young man wearing a tweed vest and white shirt. "Checking in?"

"We don't have a reservation," I said. "Do you have a vacancy?"

"Sure." He clicked on his computer. "I've got a standard king room on the second floor."

"Two rooms," Cash corrected, digging out his wallet to slap a credit card on the counter.

I shifted for my purse to fetch my own.

The clerk's gaze volleyed between the two of us. He was probably wondering if we'd just gotten into a lover's spat.

Nope. Definitely not lovers.

He finished checking us in and with room keys in hand, Cash and I walked to the elevator bank.

I reached for the button, he did too, and our fingers jabbed the up arrow at the same time. It was nothing more than a simple brush of the fingers, something we'd done a hundred times—going for the remote, flipping on a light, reaching for a set of keys—but Cash jerked away from me like I was leprous. Was my touch really that revolting?

The metallic taste of blood filled my mouth again as I bit at my cheek once more. But I would not cry, not over Cash. As much as I wanted to blame him for this, it was my fault. I'd gone too far in the car. And if I was honest with myself, none of this would have happened had I not gone too far with my heart.

We stepped into the elevator, taking opposite ends of

the car. Two floors felt like eleven and the doors were slow to open.

Cash bolted through them the moment they were wide enough to accommodate his broad shoulders. He took the lead down the hallway, bags in hand, while I followed behind, eyes aimed at the maroon and gold paisley carpet.

He set my caramel leather suitcase beside my room and without a word disappeared to his own.

Tears flooded my eyes, blurring my vision as I slid my key card into the slot. The stupid light blinked red. I did it again. Red again. "Come on," I whispered.

Finally, on the third try, when the first tear escaped, the green light blinked and I shoved my way inside. The moment the door closed behind me, I dropped my suitcase to the floor and my face into my hands. My teeth clamped together, keeping the sobs inside, but the tears were harder to control.

Why were we fighting? We never fought. Why couldn't he have let me go on this trip alone?

I would have come home and everything would have been fine. I would have broached the topic of moving out after I actually had a place to go. Because now, we'd go home and walk around each other on eggshells while I packed to leave.

Sucking in a breath, I stood straight and closed my eyes. This was only a hiccup. Today was rough. Tomorrow would be better. I sniffled and darted into the bathroom to blow my nose and dry my eyes. Then I met my gaze in the mirror.

"You're a mess." I laughed at my reflection. My hair was in a bun because I hadn't washed it this morning. My nose was puffy and my eyes were red. Tomorrow I'd take a little extra care.

I walked out of the bathroom, planning on calling home to check in. I'd waste a couple of hours, give Cash some space to cool down, then I'd go to his room and invite him for dinner, where I'd apologize and beg for his forgiveness.

He was still my friend.

I was rifling through my purse when a knock came at the door. I froze, not sure I wanted to answer it. There was no doubt it was Cash, but if he saw me, he'd know I'd been crying.

He knocked again. He'd keep knocking, and there was no use delaying my apology.

I crossed the room, double checked the peephole, then opened the door. "I'm sor—"

Before I could finish, he took a long step into the room. His hands came to my face, his palms cupping my cheeks.

And then Cash, my best friend, kissed me.

CHAPTER SEVEN

CASH

Why wasn't this awkward?

It should have been. Kissing Kat should have killed any delusions that there was chemistry between us. This kiss was a test. I'd marched over here from my room to prove that there was no spark. What better way to shove Kat firmly into the friend zone than to kiss her and cringe?

Except there was no cringe. There were no alarm bells that this was wrong. And there was definitely no desire to stop.

Kat's pink lips were soft and supple. Her face was the perfect shape for my hands, and when I licked the seam of her lips, she gasped and let me sweep my tongue inside.

Goddamn, she tasted good, like sweet peaches and mint.

I shuffled us backward into the room and the door

slammed closed behind me, but I didn't care about anything except this kiss.

Katherine's hands slid up my chest as she rose on her toes, lifting to meet me. Why wasn't she slapping me away? Why did her tongue dart out to tangle with mine?

Who fucking cares?

I was kissing a gorgeous, incredible woman and—*holy hell*—it was hot. I angled my head, dropping my hands from her face to wrap my arms around her body, and I hauled her to my chest, lifting her off the floor.

Her toes dangled above the carpet and one of her flip-flops slid free with a thud. Kat's arms were trapped between us but she wiggled them free to loop around my neck.

So there was something here. I wasn't the only one who'd felt it. The way she kissed me back, melting into my arms, there was no denying she wanted me too.

This trip. This fucking trip.

It was going to ruin us.

As I plundered her mouth, I couldn't find the will to care.

My tongue explored every corner of her mouth, tasting and sucking, until I was dizzy. The bed beckoned, drawing me closer, and without thinking twice, I laid Kat down, giving her my weight.

Her legs parted and even though she was small, I fit there. Above her. Around her. I molded my body to hers as she gave me everything she had.

How had I not noticed her before this trip? My skin tingled and electricity shot through my veins, all from her touch. How had I missed this?

Maybe I hadn't. Maybe I'd turned a blind eye to the charge between us because this was Katherine. My Kat. We weren't supposed to be kissing.

That rational thought flittered out of my mind as I sank deeper into her embrace. Never in my life had a kiss been this intense or consuming. The spark wasn't just a flicker, it was a wildfire that might destroy us both, leaving nothing but ash and destruction in its wake.

Still, I couldn't stop. I couldn't bring myself to pull away from her delicious mouth. For every second I kissed her, the heat intensified until I was panting and desperate to feel her skin, sweaty and sticky, against my own.

Finally, when I was seconds away from tearing at her top, I tore my lips away and propped up on my arms.

Fuck, but she was beautiful. Katherine's lips were red and swollen. Her cheeks were flushed and her eyes hooded.

Beneath my jeans, my erection strained painfully against the zipper. One more kiss like that and I'd make good use of this hotel room.

"Tell me to stop," I whispered. Because I couldn't do it on my own. "Tell me to go."

She shook her head. "Don't go."

Fuck. Me.

"Kat, I . . ."

What? I wasn't even sure what I wanted to say, I just knew there had to be talking.

Her hand came to my cheek, her fingertips brushing through my beard. She arched her hips, pressing her core into my hard cock, and moaned. If she liked the beard, I was never shaving again.

"Are you sure about this?" I asked.

Her eyes locked with mine and those sky-blue orbs stole my breath. "No. Are you?"

"Yes."

Yes, I was sure. Maybe tomorrow common sense and history would muddy the waters, but right here in this moment, I was sure that I'd never wanted another woman the way I wanted Kat.

She blinked and her hand fell away from my face.

"I'll go. Tell me to go," I repeated. If she wasn't sure about this, if her brain was working better than mine, I'd leave this room instantly.

Kat answered by pushing up on an elbow, closing the space between us and smashing her lips to mine.

I circled her in my arms and didn't think twice. My tongue dueled with hers and I sent a relieved groan down her throat. The one that followed was sheer lust.

She clawed at me as I clung to her. Her hands roamed the plane of my chest as I let mine knead the slight curves of her hips.

When I moved, she moved, the two of us so in sync it was like we'd been dancing around one another for years, off beat, and finally, the rhythm was coming together. Like when a rider and a horse finally found their stride.

It was fucking perfection.

"Cash." Katherine broke away from my lips to push up, forcing me to my side.

Oh, fuck. Please don't tell me to go. I would. I'd never disrespect a woman's wishes, especially Kat's, but it would be torture to return to my own room. "What?"

"Off." Her fingers grappled with the buttons on my shirt as she did her best to strip it from my shoulders.

I sat up and her hands fell away as I worked the shirt free, wanting to rip it to shreds but I didn't have a lot of spares. I yanked it from my arms and tossed it aside, reaching behind my neck to whip the undershirt away.

Katherine watched as I came down on top of her once more. Her fingertips dug into my skin, dipping and tracing between the lines of my abs. The ferocity of her touch sent a rush of heat to my throbbing cock, and I closed my eyes, praying for the shreds of my self-control to hold together.

No matter what, I'd make this good for her. I wasn't the kind of man who chased around. I dated women and even then, I rarely jumped immediately into bed. For Kat, I'd pull out all the stops because she deserved my very best.

One knee at a time, I eased my way down the bed and away from her hungry fingers. My hand dove beneath the hem of her shirt, revealing her smooth, silky skin. I dropped my mouth to her body, letting my lips skim down the centerline of her stomach until I hit the waistband of her jeans.

I tugged the button open and slid down the zipper as my feet found their way to the floor. Her jeans stripped easily from her legs and I tossed them aside, swallowing hard at the sight of her black lace panties.

Kat's toned legs were sexy as hell. How had I not noticed them before? I skimmed my fingers up her ankles, past the underside of her knees, until I had the sides of her panties in my fists. Then I dragged them off her skin, one agonizing inch at a time.

My heart beat too hard in my chest and the tightness in my ribs was painful. My cock wept, she was so stunning.

Her gaze was waiting when I forced my eyes away from her slick and bare center. Her lower lip was worried between her teeth. Kat didn't get nervous much but biting her lip was a telltale sign.

"You're perfect. You are so fucking perfect."

A flush crept up her cheeks and a smile stretched across her face. "Oh my God." Kat laughed, slapping a hand over her face to shield her eyes. "Take your pants off."

I grinned. "Yes, ma'am."

My cock sprang free as I toed off my boots and shoved my jeans and boxers down my thighs. I gripped the shaft, giving it a tug and using my thumb to spread the bead at the tip across the head.

Soon. Soon I was going to ease my cock inside Kat's body and hear her gasp my name.

Her eyes were still covered and the blush in her cheeks was spreading. I took her unaware and wrapped my hands around her ankles, earning a squeal as I jerked her to the edge of the bed. Then I dropped to my knees. Her pussy was there, glistening pink and begging for a lick.

"Cash—"

I ran my tongue through her folds.

"Oh, Cash." She arched off the bed, her hips tilting up for my mouth.

She tasted so fucking good. Sweet and hot and wet. My cock ached but before I sank into her body, I wanted her loose and ready.

I latched on to her clit and gave it a good suck, then slid a finger inside. "Wet for me, sweetheart?"

Kat moaned and fisted the covers at her sides. Her eyes were squeezed shut and her legs trembled as I found her sensitive spot and stroked. Over and over I sucked, adding another finger until she squirmed.

When her orgasm broke, it was mesmerizing. The flush on her chest. The way her body writhed against my touch. The part of her mouth and the sheer ecstasy on her beautiful face. Kat cried out and her body shook as I stared, hypnotized.

Finally, she collapsed on the mattress, limp, and I shoved up off my knees and wiped my lips dry.

I bent to fish my wallet from the pocket of my jeans,

fumbling through it for the condom I kept in case. With it rolled over my erection, I eased onto the bed.

Her eyelids were heavy as I took her under the arms and hauled her into the pillows before settling into the cradle of her hips. Kat's dark hair spread everywhere, the silky strands a beautiful contrast against the white cotton.

I brushed a hair from her eyes. "Good?"

"So. Good," she panted.

I tugged at her shirt, bringing it over her head. Then I unclasped her bra and peeled it down her arms so I could get a glimpse of her naked. God, she really was perfect. I cupped her breasts in my palms. "Ready for another one?"

The corner of her mouth turned up. "Show me what you've got, Greer."

Damn, I loved it when she challenged me. Kat had a feisty, teasing, competitive nature that she didn't often show. It was a thrill to see it in bed, to see how she'd push when I pulled.

I dragged the tip of my cock through her folds, then I positioned it at her entrance and held those blue pools as I inched inside.

She gasped and looked down to where we were joined. Her eyes widened at the sight of me stretching her, filling her.

I rocked gently, careful to give her time to adjust, and when I was as deep as I could go, she moaned, taking her knees in her hands to spread them wider.

"Fuck, that is hot."

She hummed her agreement.

I eased out and thrust inside, earning a hitch of breath and a coy smile. My mental notebook of what it took to create Kat's whimpers and moans was filling up fast. Maybe today was the exception, but damn it, I hoped I'd get to experiment again.

Sunlight streamed through the windows as we moved together, bringing one another higher and higher. Kat's hands were like butterfly wings, brushing over the sensitive places on my torso and hips and shoulders and ass. They fluttered, driving me wild.

She rolled her hips with my strokes, that push and pull better than I could have imagined. Missionary with Katherine Gates was fucking erotic. She really was something special. I'd known it outside this room but add the sexy and wanton woman screwing me senseless, and she was like the rarest of diamonds, shining only for me.

The threat of reality caught the edge of my consciousness, tapping on my shoulder to remind me that this was my best friend I was fucking. Had I ruined us? Had this just destroyed the one friendship I held above all others?

I shoved those thoughts away. For today. For tomorrow. Forever. Later, I'd think about how everything between us would change.

Bending down, I sucked at the column of her throat. Her fingers threaded into the longer strands of my hair at the nape, tugging them with just enough pressure that I grinned and nipped at the underside of her jaw.

"Harder," she moaned.

I let loose, pistoning my hips faster and faster. Slamming us together until the sound of skin slapping against skin was probably audible in the hallway. My kisses on her bare skin became frantic. I pinched one of her nipples, then enveloped the hard bud in my mouth.

Kat arched, her grip on my hair as tight as ever.

We fucked, hard and so, so good, and when her second orgasm broke, I didn't try to hold back. Pleasure shot down my spine and I tightened, letting my release take over. Wave after wave, I groaned through every pulse of her inner walls squeezing and draining me dry, until I was wrecked.

My heart hammered inside my chest as I eased out of her body to collapse by her side. My legs were shaking and my arms boneless.

Kat sprawled on the bed, her breathing as ragged as my own. We were sweaty and sticky, just like I'd wanted.

And for one last, brief moment, I didn't think about what was to come. The unavoidable conversation. I took her hand in mine and held it like she was my lover.

That short moment was all I got.

Kat shot off the bed, blinking and shoving her hair out of her face. "I, um . . ."

Instead of finishing her sentence, she spun around and raced for the bathroom. The spray of the shower's water sounded after the door's lock clicked.

I brought my hands to my face, rubbing away the sex fog. Then I pushed up to a seat, peeling off the condom.

Fuck. What did this mean? Never in my life had I connected with a woman like that. It was . . . my mind was too hazy to come up with the right word. Phenomenal wasn't strong enough.

I stood on shaking legs and took the condom to the trash can, then sat on the end of the bed, hanging my head forward.

I wouldn't regret it. Even if Kat said it was a mistake and she wanted to just be friends again, fine. But I wouldn't regret it.

Maybe we could . . . I wasn't sure what I wanted.

To date? That sounded cheap for someone like Kat. All I knew was that I'd never be able to look at her the same way again. I'd always see her naked and wild beneath me. For a short time, she'd given me that trust.

Before bolting from the bed like she couldn't wait to rinse me from her skin.

The sound of my phone ringing jolted me from my stupor and I bent, plucking it from my jeans.

Grandma.

"What's up?" I answered, trapping the phone between my ear and my shoulder so I could pull on my boxers.

"Well, hello to you too, grandson. Yes, I'm doing well. Thanks for asking."

"Great. You're welcome."

She laughed. "Smartass."

"Learned from the best."

"I was just calling to check in. See how you are doing."

"We're fine." *Fan-fucking-tastic.* But it wasn't like I could tell Grandma that I was totally messed up over my best friend, who was currently in the shower.

"Good. With that out of the way, I have something to tell you."

My heart stopped. "What? Is everyone okay?"

"Oh, yes. Everyone is fine. Your dad is covering for you at the facility."

I rolled my eyes. There was nothing to cover. None of the questions left unanswered had to be solved immediately. We hadn't even started construction. Dad had just jumped at the chance to make some decisions without any interference.

Whatever. If I didn't like something, I'd just change it later.

"Nice of him to do that," I said. "What did you have to tell me?"

"That trip wasn't for you, Cash."

I blinked and stood tall. "What?"

"You should be at home."

"Work will wait two weeks. Besides, it's not like I'm a critical component." Yet.

Kat had been onto something in the car. Something I *never* spoke about. Something I rarely mentally acknowledged.

For the past decade, since I'd graduated college, I'd

been treated more like an employee at the Greer ranch than the owner I was.

The only consolation was that the family dynamics were hard for Easton too. Which was why I had been pissed when he'd gone ahead and bought property for the training facility without asking.

But what was I supposed to do? Fight with him about it? I was getting my dream job. Not in the way I'd wanted it, but once the expansion happened, did it matter?

"I'm not talking about work," Grandma said. "That was Katherine's trip to get away."

"I wasn't going to let her drive off alone. It was a dangerous idea from the beginning."

She scoffed. "Katherine is tougher than any person I know."

Grandma wasn't wrong. "Then maybe I wanted a break too."

"But it's not about you."

"Okay." Where the hell was she going with this?

"You don't get it."

"Then explain it to me."

She sighed. "Just don't dictate how the trip is going to go."

"I'm not."

She scoffed again. "Yeah, right. I know you. You'll play the big brother and suddenly Kat's vacation will be yours."

I was *not* her brother. I gritted my teeth together. "Anything else?"

"Just . . . give her the chance to explore. To think."

"Think about what?" What the fuck was Grandma talking about?

"About the future."

My heart stopped. Was this about Kat moving out? Had she already told Grandma? Or was there more?

I was missing something. A big something. But what?

I'd thought this trip was for Kat to take a break from working twelve-hour days and to reconnect with an old friend, but as the days had progressed, the unease in my gut had begun to brew like an angry storm.

I was losing her.

My gut screamed that I was losing her.

The water from the shower stopped and the curtain scraped across its rod. "Bye, Grandma."

Without waiting for her response, I ended the call and tossed the phone aside. Then I wadded up my jeans and shirts and picked up my boots, taking them to the closed bathroom door. "Kat?"

"Yeah?" she called back.

"I'm going to go back to my room. Take a shower."

"O-okay."

"Do you want to meet for dinner?" I held my breath, unsure if I wanted the answer to be yes or no.

Before Grandma's call, I would have insisted, but her warning, the way this trip had been going, something had me on edge. Maybe I'd been pushing Kat too hard.

Like my grandmother had said, it wasn't about me.

I stood, waiting for her answer. The water from the shower dripped and dripped. Finally, she said, "No."

No.

What the fuck had we done?

I walked out of her room and into mine, knowing things would never be the same.

CHAPTER EIGHT

KATHERINE

Pathetic. Idiotic. Reckless. Pretty much any way I studied what had happened between me and Cash yesterday, there wasn't a positive adjective to be found.

Cash had kissed me.

Cash had kissed me *everywhere*. I should have been elated. I should have been laughing and happy. For years, I'd dreamed that he'd take notice and just *kiss me*.

Wish granted.

Except now I felt like a fool.

Thank God I'd disappeared to the shower to hide my happy tears yesterday.

I'd used the five-minute shower after we'd had sex to compose myself. To have my quick, squealing fit of joy. Cash had worshiped me. There was no other way to describe it. He'd made my body come alive.

As I'd stood under the spray, I'd worked up the

courage to tell Cash how I felt. To tell him I wanted more than his friendship.

I was grateful that he'd left before then. I hadn't had to witness him re-dress and leave. He'd saved me from an extravagant rejection. Part of me wanted to be furious with him. Mostly, I was ashamed.

Did he know I had feelings for him? I'd thought my hug from the first night had tipped him off, but maybe I'd guessed wrong. Maybe he'd just been in a strange mood. But if he didn't know I had feelings for him, why come to my room yesterday? Why have sex with me? Mind-numbing, toe-curling, soul-shattering sex.

The right thing to do would be to talk about it, but we hadn't spoken. Not one word since he'd left my room. There'd been no hello in the hotel lobby this morning. When I'd come down to check out, he'd been in the lounge area adjacent to the front desk—bag packed, ball cap on and ready to leave.

I was too scared to bring it up. Reliving painful experiences through conversation wasn't my favorite pastime and Cash walking out on me yesterday had been excruciating.

Yesterday's drive had been awful. Horrifically awful. It paled in comparison to today's.

We'd arrive in Heron Beach today and though I was nervous to see Aria after all this time, I could hardly wait for another person to buffer the conversation.

But first . . . the apology I'd planned to give Cash was still overdue. And the truth was, I needed Cash today.

I needed him by my side when I saw Aria.

What if she'd changed for the worse since our parting at the junkyard? What if her life was in shambles? It would break my heart. My reunion with Gemma had been different. *She'd* found *me*, and we'd been on my turf. What if Aria didn't want to see me, or worse, remember me?

I clutched the steering wheel and took a deep breath. I was the general manager of a multimillion-dollar resort. I'd earned the position without a college degree or professional training. I could mend fences with my best friend.

"I'm sorry about yesterday," I said. "For what I said in the car."

Cash looked over and gave me a small smile. "Me too."

"I don't want to fight."

"Kat." My name sounded pained and his voice hoarse. He blew out a long breath. "Yesterday. In your room. I—"

"What if we don't talk about it?" Because if he wanted to forget it, if he wanted to pretend like it hadn't happened, my heart would break. So I'd say it first. "What if we forget it ever happened?"

"No."

I blinked, glancing over at him. His jaw was tight. His hazel eyes waiting. "What do you mean?"

"It happened, Kat. I don't want to forget."

"Then what do you want?"

"Truth? I have no fucking clue."

"Me neither." I sighed, so unbelievably relieved he didn't have an answer. That he didn't want to forget about me.

"You're my best friend. The reason I was so pissed in the car yesterday was because you're right. I don't want to admit you're right. Sometimes, it's easier to shut it off."

"I understand." After all, I did the same thing. But this . . . this wasn't my mother or my childhood that I could avoid. I saw Cash every single day. "We had sex. This changes everything."

"Yeah, it does." He nodded. "But today's a big day. Let's get through it. Find Aria."

"Shut it off."

"For today."

I breathed another sigh, this one of gratitude. I could use a day or two off to let yesterday's emotions simmer.

"How's today going to go?" Cash asked.

I shrugged. "I don't know."

"Nervous?"

"Yes. I'm sneaking up on her with this car idea. We had an investigator look into her life. She might not remember me or appreciate that I've searched her out."

"I think you're worrying for nothing. It'll be good." He reached over, his finger ready to flick the tip of my nose, a gesture he'd done a thousand times, but before he touched me, he retracted his hand.

I tried not to let it hurt.

Cash rubbed his bearded jaw. "Grandma called yesterday while you were in the shower."

"Oh." Carol would call him but not me? I'd tried her, Liddy and Gemma last night and no one had answered. No one had returned a single one of my texts or voicemails. What the hell? Didn't anyone miss me? It made sense why'd they'd call Cash. He was real family. I was the employee on vacation.

"She just wanted to check in."

"That's good. Did she say anything about work?"

"No."

My heart sank. I put out metaphorical fires daily at the resort. Didn't anyone need my help? How was it that I ran myself ragged for days but no one had reached out? No one. Not even Carol.

But that meant she was handling it. I was replaceable.

It wasn't something I wanted to admit.

Work was my life and without it, who was I? The friends I had were from the resort. Everyone in my life was connected to the Greers. I hadn't dated a man in seven years because I hadn't had—or made—time.

I'd been so focused on the tiny sphere of my world that I'd forgotten there was more beyond.

And what a beautiful world.

The highway had been bordered by thick bushes, limiting the view beyond the road. But as the Cadillac crested the top of a hill, the greenery cleared and there it was.

Heron Beach. Beyond the town, the ocean stretched. White, foamy waves broke against a smooth, sandy beach. On the horizon, blue sky met the Pacific, gray waters and the colors blurring into an ombre line.

"I've never seen the ocean," I whispered, my eyes trapped on the view. The car slowed as I pulled my foot from the accelerator, wanting more time to savor this view. I rolled down my window, wanting to feel the air on my face. The salty air filled my nostrils and I held it in my lungs.

"Really?" Cash asked. "What about California?"

"No." Temecula was an inland town and it wasn't like Mom had believed in mother-daughter vacations to the beach. "It's beautiful."

And suddenly, Montana's firm hold, the grip it had caught me with at eighteen, began to loosen.

What if I didn't live and work in Montana my entire life? What if I gave Oregon a try? I could see myself living here, walking along the beach each morning with a dog who chased his own tail. I could ride a bike with a wicker basket around the quaint, small town. Maybe one of the beach condos would fit into my price range.

Before this trip, I'd never had a desire to travel the world. To smell new scents. To explore new towns. All I'd ever wanted was to carve out a place to stay.

A home.

Londyn had set out in the Cadillac to run away. She'd

wanted to create a new life and she'd found one in West Virginia. Gemma had found her place in Montana.

What if I'd been thinking about this all wrong? This trip was for me to clear my head and put my feelings for Cash aside. What if this wasn't a vacation, but my own fresh start?

The idea startled me. I blinked, forcing it away.

No. No way. I couldn't leave Montana.

Except I could.

"Cool place," Cash said, sitting straighter in his seat and pulling me from the craziest idea I'd had in years— crazier even than sex with my best friend.

I hummed my agreement.

From a distance, Heron Beach was exactly as I would have pictured an ocean tourist destination. My foot pressed on the gas, ready to see it up close. As we dipped down the hill, the ocean dropped out of view, hidden by the trees towering above. Buildings sprouted along the highway.

I followed the signs into town, slowing as we hit more traffic near the coast. The downtown streets of Heron Beach teemed with people who smiled as they wandered and shopped.

Flowerpots overflowed with florescent blooms. Sun-soaked shingles covered nearly every storefront. Most businesses were retailers who probably flourished this time of year with the crush of tourists. The hotels along the way were small, likely with a capacity of ten to fifteen guests.

None were as grand as the Greer Ranch and Mountain Resort but they had a different kind of charm. I could own a hotel of that size on my own. I'd been saving for years and my nest egg would probably be enough for an oceanfront cottage. And I had that check Carol had given me for ten thousand dollars.

"Where are we going?" Cash asked, again dragging me back to reality.

I picked up Gemma's sticky note that I'd set on the dash earlier, rereading the hotel's name. "The Gallaway."

He dug his phone from his pocket and entered the hotel's name into the GPS.

I followed its directions through Heron Beach until a grand hotel, one that could compete with even the Greers' establishment, filled the view. "Wow."

Four stories of taupe siding trimmed in white. Gleaming windows that offered guests a magnificent view of the ocean roaring in the distance. The Gallaway sat on a rocky cliff—twenty feet of jagged, charcoal rock that dropped to flawless, golden sand.

The hotel's parking loop was tall and wide enough to accommodate a tour bus and two stretch limos with room in between. I pulled the Cadillac to the curb and before I could touch the handle to open the door, a valet was at my side.

"Welcome to The Gallaway."

"Thank you." I stepped out, smiling as I took in the entrance.

The front doors were open and the floor's stones were made of the palest gray. Any accent was done in white or gold to keep the ambience bright and airy.

Everything in Montana was decorated with dark tones and earthy pieces. I'd finally gotten so sick of the wood that when Carol had given me the thumbs-up to make some enhancements, I'd added light touches wherever possible. From upholstered dining room chairs to freshly painted walls to quilts and pillowcases. Any surface where I'd been able to swap a shade of brown or maroon for something cream or white, I hadn't hesitated.

Cash met the bellhop at the trunk. The poor kid tried to retrieve our sparse luggage, but Cash shot him a look of dismissal. *He carried the bags. Got it.*

I rolled my eyes and dug for Carol's quarter I'd tossed aside earlier. I found it and set it in the metal ashtray, then hooked my purse over a shoulder and handed the keys to the valet. My eyes traced over every detail from the over-flowing planters that bracketed the entrance to the gold *G* embedded in the stone tile beneath the entrance's threshold.

If the entrance was this nice, I couldn't wait to see the guest rooms. I'd be taking mental notes during our stay of things we could incorporate at the lodge.

Cash glanced over his shoulder to where the valet was easing the Cadillac through the loop. "I hate valet. Always screwing something up with your vehicle. Don't be surprised if we get it back with a scratch."

"He's not going to scratch the car."

We didn't have valet at the resort because we didn't cater to mass numbers of guests. At most, we had ten to fifteen cars in the parking lot. Most guests flew into Missoula and our shuttle service brought them to the property. We offered an experience, not a luxurious hotel that turned guests over by the hundreds.

The lobby was as stunning as the entrance, with gleaming marble floors and a chandelier that hung low, its crystal facets fracturing the light everywhere into tiny rainbows.

I spun in a slow circle, taking it all in before Cash nudged me toward the front desk.

The blonde behind the counter greeted us with a wide smile. "Welcome to The Gallaway."

"Thank you."

"Name?" she asked, fingers poised above her keyboard.

I scrunched up my nose. "We don't have a reservation. Do you have any rooms available by chance?"

"Oooh." The woman cringed. "Um . . . let me see what I can find. We're at the beginning of peak season so I'm not sure if we have any openings."

Why hadn't I called ahead? Oh, that's right. Because this trip had been a whirlwind and the situation with Cash had occupied my every waking thought. I crossed my fingers, hoping as the receptionist's nails clicked on keys that she'd find us a room. I really didn't want to find another place to stay but the chance of a vacancy was slim if the activity in the lobby was any indication of occupancy.

People streamed in and out from what looked like a long deck on the back of the hotel that overlooked the ocean. Some carried coffee cups from the espresso bar located past a set of french doors. Others milled around in the gift shop.

"Ah, you're in luck." My heart soared as the blonde's smile widened. "I've got one standard king room available. It's a garden view room on the first floor."

No. Damn. I needed to start leading with the number of rooms. "We actually need two rooms so—"

"We'll take it." Cash pulled out his wallet.

I should argue and insist on a hotel with two rooms. Things were tense enough as it was without us sharing a bed, but this place was a hotel resort manager's dream.

The woman's fingers flew as she checked us in. The smile on her face never faltered, even when Cash grumbled at the price.

I leaned close to whisper. "You do realize how much we charge, don't you?"

"Garden view," he whispered back.

Staying at the Greer lodge cost thousands of dollars per night. For the chalets, we charged a premium. It was the reason we catered to the wealthy and famous. With our on-site amenities, excursions and gourmet food from Chef Wong, we offered an experience you couldn't find anywhere else.

Paying four hundred dollars for a garden view room was nothing. Besides, it wasn't like Cash was hurting for money.

With our key cards in hand, I picked up my suitcase from where Cash had rested it on the floor. I turned away from the desk only to remember why I was here and whirled back around to the clerk. "Could I trouble you for one more thing? I'm looking for Aria Saint-James. We're old friends."

"Would you like me to page her? I can have her call your room."

Gemma's private investigator had done his job well. "That would be great. Thanks."

When I turned away again, expecting to see Cash behind me, he was gone. I scanned the area and spotted him just before he stepped out onto the deck so I hurried to catch up.

The moment I stepped outside onto gray-stained boards, the smell of the sea encircled me. The scent of a fresh Montana spring morning was hard to beat, with its green grass and cold mountain mix. But this was invigorating. The breeze rushed past my face, cooling my skin. The gulls crowed above our heads.

I joined Cash at the deck's railing and soaked in the view. The ocean stretched before us and in that moment, I didn't mind feeling small.

Waves rushed to the sand, breaking and fizzling as they faded away. The shores were full of people walking in bare feet, the water erasing their footprints as it rushed to the beach.

I shielded my eyes from the sun and scoped out the deck. They'd filled the space with Adirondack chairs, chaise lounges and white benches. Between the seats were pots of blooming flowers and spilling foliage.

Someone here had a green thumb. I suspected who and had a feeling the garden view wouldn't be so bad.

The ocean's calming rush soothed away the tension from the trip. Now that Cash and I weren't cramped together in the Cadillac, it was easier to breathe. I dropped my suitcase at my feet to lean my forearms on the railing.

Cash stood with his hands shoved in his jeans pockets. He stared at the water, his eyebrows two dark slashes above narrowed eyes.

"What's wrong?"

He sniffed the air. "It stinks like fish."

I laughed. "For a man who spends most of his days around cow pies and horse apples, I didn't realize you were so sensitive to smell."

He shot me a scowl, then glanced over his shoulder to take in the hotel's backside. His chin tipped up as he scrutinized the four floors and their balconies above. "I bet the standard room is half the size of ours at the lodge."

"Probably." We lived in Big Sky Country and the resort's standard rooms were the most spacious I'd ever seen.

"Four hundred bucks." He scoffed. "What a rip-off."

"You didn't have so many complaints about the last two hotels."

Not that he would. It was no contest. His problem with The Gallaway was that this place could offer some competition and he was in a shit mood.

Cash was normally a cheerful man who wore a smile often and laughed in earnest. But he was a Greer and not only were they stubborn, they had a grouchy streak that ran deep.

"Should we go somewhere else?" I asked.

"No." He bent to pick up my suitcase. "Let's go see our *garden view*."

I shook my head, blowing out a long breath. If he wanted to sulk, I'd leave him in our room and go explore the ocean alone.

As we reentered the lobby, I noticed more of the classic details. They'd put mirrors on the walls instead of art, making the space seem larger. Every other glass door was monogramed with the same *G* as the entrance.

Cash led the way and before disappearing into the alcove with the elevators, I took one last glance at the lobby. A door behind the receptionist desk opened and a man in a charcoal suit emerged.

He was tall with broad shoulders and a trim physique. He spoke over his shoulder and when the woman he'd been addressing emerged from beyond the door, my hand slapped over my heart.

Her hair was a shade darker than I remembered but

her smile was exactly the same, mischievous and daring. The man said something that made her laugh and her shining brown eyes drifted through the lobby as she followed him around the counter. Her gaze swept past me, then snapped back, just as Cash appeared at my side.

She blinked, then that infectious smile spread across her face.

"Are you coming?" Cash asked, his gaze following mine. "Wait, is that—"

"Aria."

CHAPTER NINE

CASH

"I cannot believe you're here." Aria laughed, shaking her head like Kat wasn't sitting beside her at the table. She'd said the same, done the same, after crushing Kat in a hug in the lobby earlier today. I've never seen two women hug so hard. The moment Kat had spotted Aria, the women had rushed toward one another, colliding in a fierce embrace.

They'd hugged again before Aria had returned to work, then again when we'd met this evening at the hotel's steakhouse.

"I know." Katherine smiled with her friend. "I was actually worried you wouldn't recognize me and I was going to have to introduce myself."

You're unforgettable. I swallowed the words. Three days ago, I could have said them and made Kat blush. They wouldn't have been anything but a friendly compliment. She would have teased me for being gooey and I would have slung an arm around her shoulders and flicked the tip of her nose.

But that was three days ago. Now a compliment wasn't simply a compliment. A compliment like that might make Kat think I was flirting. That it was foreplay. Maybe it was.

Maybe it had always been.

"I'd never forget you." Aria put her hand over Kat's, then let her go to pick up the menu. "I'm starved. I haven't eaten here in a while but I always leave full."

"Any recommendations?" I asked.

"The steaks are incredible," she said.

"Sold." I closed my menu and set it aside. Steak was a staple in my diet and as a co-owner of a large Montana cattle ranch, I supported the beef industry whenever possible. But I doubted The Gallaway could deliver a filet I could slice with my fork.

This place was too pretentious. Kat was fascinated with the hotel but something about the place made me uneasy. Maybe it was because I'd never seen her so awestruck. Our resort was ten times better, so why was she drooling over everything?

Kat ran her finger down the stem of her water goblet. "I love these."

Of course she did. Which meant in a month, the resort would have all new water goblets.

The scrape of silverware on plates and dull conversation filled the room. There wasn't an empty table in sight. Waiters bustled around wearing white-collared shirts and black vests. Our dining room staff was only required to wear slacks and a button-up with the resort logo on the breast pocket. If Kat made them don a vest, we'd have a riot in the staff quarters.

"Sorry I couldn't meet with you earlier," Aria said. "We're right at the beginning of peak season and I've been swamped now that the rain has finally stopped and everything is in full bloom."

"No problem," Kat said. "I should have called first."

"I'm glad you didn't." Aria folded up her menu and set it on top of mine. "I love surprises."

Katherine giggled. "You haven't changed."

"My sister says that all the time." Aria leaned her elbows on the table. "What did you do today?"

Kat glanced at me, finally remembering I was sitting at the table too. "Not much. We did some exploring around town."

After Kat and Aria's reunion, Aria had returned to work while Katherine and I had dropped off our luggage in our room. One look at the bed and Kat had tossed her suitcase aside and announced she wanted to go shopping.

I hated shopping but it was better than staying in that room alone, dwelling on yesterday.

What were we going to do?

Part of me wanted to explore this thing, see if we were as combustible in bed a second and third time. But the other part of me longed to cling to our friendship and do everything in my damn power to put us back to normal.

I didn't want to lose her.

If we tried this thing, if we failed, I'd lose Kat.

"It's a cute town, isn't it?" Aria asked.

Kat nodded. "So cute."

It was just okay. After we'd dropped off our bags and I'd surveyed the room—as I'd expected, it was nice but smaller than any of our guest rooms—we'd left the hotel to wander downtown.

The sidewalks had been crowded with visitors like us. She'd been interested in the stores but completely engrossed with every bed and breakfast that we'd passed. We'd popped into a few shops and she'd bought some souvenirs to take home.

The town's economy was clearly driven by tourism. There were knickknack displays on every block. For fifty dollars, Kat had bought a pale blue glass jar filled with *authentic Oregon seashells* as a gift to Mom. Easton and Gemma were getting a driftwood coaster set. She'd picked up T-shirts for Dad and Granddad, then a postcard for Grandma.

She knew that my grandma didn't love trinkets, so instead, she'd decided to send a postcard that Grandma would receive before we ever got home. She'd written a note on it when we'd arrived at the room before dinner, then had disappeared to find a stamp. The task had taken her up until the very moment she'd come back to the room to change clothes and get ready for dinner with Aria.

As she'd searched for the mysterious stamp, I'd unsuccessfully tried to nap. I hadn't gotten much sleep in last night's hotel room, not with Katherine's scent lingering on my skin and her taste on my lips. But sleep was difficult with so much unknown swirling in my mind.

Every thought was consumed with Kat.

I stared at her as she browsed the menu. It was impossible not to think of how she'd felt in my arms and how her smooth skin had felt pressed against mine. She was wearing a pair of skintight jeans and sandals. Her top was another silky piece with thin straps that I'd never seen before and its rust color made her eyes vividly blue.

I forced my eyes away to the silverware resting on a pressed white napkin. When I glanced up, looking anywhere but at Kat, Aria's eyes were waiting.

Aria was taller than Kat—most people were. Her hair was dark and her eyes warm with a slightly cunning edge. She smiled effortlessly but there was a hesitancy behind her gaze. Either she was sizing me up or she held people at bay.

Probably both.

The waiter arrived with a bottle of wine and he poured Kat the sample. She sipped it, then nodded and lifted the glass for more. After he'd made the rounds, filling our glasses, he took our order and then left us to talk.

"Tell me about your life." Aria shifted in her seat to

face Kat, giving her friend her undivided attention. "How was Montana?"

"Good. I'm still there, working at the resort."

"Not just working," I corrected. "She's the manager. Kat runs the whole show."

Katherine blushed. "Not exactly."

"Yes, exactly." Why was she being modest? She'd accomplished so much, made so many improvements to the resort. I, along with every member of my family, was amazed at what she'd accomplished in the span of a few years.

Systems were streamlined. Guest satisfaction had never been higher. The staff was happy and turnover was at an all-time low. It was because of Kat and I was damn proud of her.

"And how did you two meet?" Aria asked.

Kat gave me a small smile and damn it if that quirk of her lips didn't make my heart skip. "Cash's family owns the ranch and resort."

"Ah. How long have you been together?"

I opened my mouth to answer but Kat beat me to it with a wave of her hand. "Oh, no. We're not together. We're just friends. And coworkers."

"Don't forget roommates." There was a bitter edge to my voice.

"And roommates," she added.

Why did it bug me that she was so quick to dismiss us as friends? We were friends. And coworkers. And roommates.

I gulped from my wineglass, hoping it would take the edge off. It was better with Aria here to defuse some of the tension, but she didn't erase it entirely. The undercurrents tugged and tormented. I should have stayed in the room and let this be a private reunion.

"Ah." Aria lifted her own glass, studying me over the rim as she took a drink. "Well, what brings you *roommates* to Oregon?"

Kat took a deep breath and a long drag of her wine before answering. She and Aria hadn't spoken in the lobby earlier, deciding to save the conversation for dinner, when it wouldn't be rushed. She set her wine down and smiled at her friend. "You, actually."

"Me? Why? I thought it was just a coincidence."

"No, not really." Katherine bit her bottom lip.

I shifted my leg, extending it beneath the table so my foot touched hers and when she looked up, I gave her a nod. For the first time since yesterday, neither of us stiffened from the touch. This, right here, was why I was at the table. Tonight, Kat needed me to be her friend.

"Okay, let me start at the beginning," Kat said. "You know that old Cadillac that Londyn lived in?"

"Yeah." Aria nodded.

"A while back, Londyn had it shipped to Boston, where she was living. She bought it from Lou and had it completely restored."

"Lou," Aria whispered. "Haven't heard that name in a

while. Did you hear that he passed? Clara found out from someone in Temecula about a year after he died."

"Yeah," Kat said. "Gemma told me."

"You've talked to Gemma?"

"She actually lives on the ranch."

"She's getting married to my brother," I added. "And bosses us all around."

Aria laughed. "Why am I not surprised? How is she?"

"She's wonderful," Kat said. "It was actually her idea that I come out here but let me back up. Londyn had the Cadillac in Boston. She'd just gone through a nasty divorce and decided to drive the Cadillac to California and find Karson. But she got a flat tire in West Virginia and ended up meeting her husband, Brooks, so the California trip never happened."

"Is she happy?" Aria asked. "Londyn?"

"Yeah." Kat smiled. "I don't talk to her often. She's closer to Gemma than me, but she's happy. They have a little girl named Ellie and she's pregnant again. Due any day now."

"That's so good to hear," Aria breathed. "I think about them, everyone, once in a while. I'm glad she's happy. Gemma too."

It had always struck me as odd that Kat hadn't kept in touch with the kids from the junkyard. After such a harrowing childhood, why wouldn't they have bonded together for life? But then again, I lived in Clear River, Montana. My graduating class had been fifteen people, most of whom still lived around the area, working on their family's farms and ranches. Kat and her friends had scattered across the country.

"Gemma was in Boston with Londyn," Kat said. "I lost touch with both of them after they left Montana, but those two stayed connected. Last year, Gemma sold her company in Boston and kind of . . . quit her life. She went to visit Londyn in West Virginia and Londyn suggested she finish the trip to California instead."

"Did she find Karson?"

Kat shook her head. "No. She came to find me in Montana. And fell in love with Easton."

My brother had told me a few months ago that he wasn't sure how he'd gotten so lucky. The day that Gemma had rolled onto the ranch in the Cadillac was the best day of his life. Granted, at the time he hadn't realized it. But after the two of them had stopped trying to tear one another's heads off—tearing clothes off instead—they hadn't been apart.

"They're having a baby boy in a few months," I said.

"And you?" Aria asked Kat. "Are you happy?"

"Of course." Kat shifted in her chair again, reaching for her wine.

My heart sank. Maybe Aria had bought the lie but I'd heard the truth in Kat's voice.

Why wasn't she happy? Didn't she like her job? Didn't she like life on the ranch? Or was it just stress from the past three days I was hearing?

"That brings me to this visit," Kat said, continuing on. "Gemma hired a PI a while back to look us all up. She was curious and wanted to know where we'd all landed. I hope you don't mind. I—we—drove the Cadillac here to find you."

"Not Karson?"

"No." Kat shook her head. "I'm never going back to California."

Because of her mother? Because of the memories? Hell if I knew the answer. More than I wanted anything from Kat, her body or her friendship, I craved her trust.

"I can understand that." Aria gulped the rest of her wine and refilled her and Kat's glasses. "I'm not going back either."

"Oh." Kat's shoulders slumped. "Damn. We were hoping that you might take the car to Karson."

"Is he in California?"

"According to Gemma's PI, yes."

Aria hummed and twirled the wine in her glass. "You know, I've thought of doing the same, with an investigator. Except for the fact that I'm a gardener and can't really afford that sort of thing."

"You're a gardener?" I asked.

Aria touched the tip of a tulip in the vase on the table. "Everything around the hotel has been grown by me or a member of my team. I cut these flowers this morning in our offsite greenhouse after I saw you in the lobby."

"I wondered about that." Kat smiled and looked to me.

"Aria was always growing things in the junkyard. She'd buy a packet of seeds and find an old egg carton. Then we'd all get a plant or a flower for our own, usually in an empty can of green beans. I was sad to leave them behind when we left."

Aria's face soured. "I hate green beans. But don't worry, I took care of your flowers. I found these industrial buckets and I made Karson help me fill them with dirt. Then I replanted everything and staged them all around the junkyard. I'll never forget the look on Lou's face when he came out of his shack one day to see all the green leaves and pink flowers I'd put beside his front door. It was this hilarious mix of shock and disgust and pride."

"Poor Lou." Kat laughed, fondness in her gaze.

Poor Lou? That man had let a bunch of kids camp out in his junkyard, living in abandoned cars and ramshackle tents. But that reverence that Katherine and Gemma had for the junkyard, for Lou, was written on Aria's face too.

"Remember that time your cat destroyed all my seedlings?" Aria asked.

"She didn't destroy them." Kat rolled her eyes. "She just knocked over a couple."

"All of them. That animal was an evil, orange beast. I still hate cats to this day."

"Did, um . . . did Lou feed her after I left?"

Aria nodded. "And all of her kittens. When I finally left the next year, there were like twenty cats living around his shack. But no mice."

"You had a cat?" I asked. Another thing I wished I had known.

"Just this stray that kept coming by." Kat shrugged. "She wasn't really mine. I fed her a few times and then she didn't leave. We didn't let her sleep in the tent with us, but she kind of gravitated toward me."

"She *only* gravitated toward you," Aria said. "That cat would hiss and scratch the rest of us if we tried to pet her."

It was strange to observe Kat with someone else from her youth. For the first time, I was the outsider. Gemma and Kat didn't talk about the junkyard. If they did, it was done at their weekly girls' night because whenever they were around the family, conversation was focused on life and happenings on the ranch.

But Aria had no connection to the Greers. I'd learned more about Kat in the past few days than I'd learned in a decade.

The waiter arrived with our dinner and conversation halted as the three of us began eating.

"Wow." Katherine's eyes widened after the first bite of her steak. "This is amazing."

I swallowed my own bite, hating to admit that it was good. I'd also cut that bite with my fork.

"Do you still paint?" Aria asked as she fluffed her baked potato.

Kat shook her head. "No, not anymore."

"You paint?" My fork froze in midair. "I didn't know that."

She shrugged and popped another bite into her mouth, chewing and avoiding eye contact.

"She's talented," Aria said. "She did this mural inside the tent of this meadow with wildflowers and birds and butterflies. It was so bright and cheerful. Whenever I had a bad day, I'd go into the tent and just lie down in the common area, close my eyes and be surrounded by the colors."

"Why'd you stop?" I asked Kat, not caring that my knowledge—or lack thereof—was showing.

"It got harder and harder to do. With work being so busy, it was one of those hobbies that fell away."

Did she have other former hobbies I didn't know about? Besides working at the resort, she didn't do much for herself. She'd go horseback riding at times. She'd hang out and watch a basketball or football game with me at home.

How had I known her all these years without knowing she'd had a cat in the junkyard or that she'd been a painter? So much for me being the all-knowing best friend.

"What happened after we left?" Katherine asked Aria.

"Nothing much. It was boring without you guys there. Karson stayed until we turned eighteen, but he wasn't around much. He worked a ton, we all did, trying to save some money. Then on our birthday, Clara and I packed up our stuff and took a bus to Las Vegas. Karson hugged us goodbye, we left a note for Lou, and that was it."

"How long were you in Vegas?"

"About a month. I hated it. Too many fake people. Too much desert. Clara liked it and stayed for a while before moving to Welcome, Arizona. But I had to get out of there. So I started calling hotels along the coast, seeing if there were any jobs open. I started as a housekeeper here at The Gallaway for about a year. Then one day, the head groundskeeper found me weeding one of the flower beds. He took me under his wing, showed me everything and taught me a lot. When he retired a few years ago, I took over."

"We both started as housekeepers then," Kat said. "That's how I started at the resort."

"What do you do, Cash?" Aria asked.

"I work with horses. I do some guide trips. Train the younger animals. Do whatever ranch work needs to be done."

"So you're a cowboy?" She leaned back to look under the table. "Boots and all."

I chuckled. "Something like that."

"Cash has a real gift with horses," Kat said. "They're building a brand-new training and breeding facility that he's going to run."

"With Gemma," I added. "She came to my rescue and saved me from the office work."

"I'll have to come and visit the resort one of these days. I'm intrigued."

"You're welcome anytime," Kat said.

Conversation turned light as the three of us focused on

our meals. Aria told some funny tales about catching couples screwing on the beach when they thought no one was looking. She raved about the hotel's owner and how he was the best boss she'd ever had and the kindest rich man she'd ever met.

When her plate was clear, Aria set her napkin aside, leaning forward to focus on Kat. "I love this visit. I love the whole idea for your trip. What if I took the Cadillac?"

"To California?" Kat asked. "I thought . . ."

"No, to Clara, in Arizona. I'll be next up in the daisy chain. Once she hears about how the handoffs have worked with the car, I'm sure she'll take it to Karson."

"Really?" Kat's face split in a huge smile.

"Sure. As long as you're not in a hurry. Work is crazy right now, but as soon as I can get away, I'll do it."

"There's no rush. For either of you. If Clara doesn't want to drive to California, we can leave the car in Arizona. Gemma will come get it at some point. Or Londyn."

"Then it's settled." Aria clapped. "Though I'm not worried about my sister. Clara will love the idea even more than me."

"Thank you," I said. Not only because that would save us a long drive home, but because of the smile she'd put on Kat's face.

"You're welcome." Aria yawned and checked the time on her phone. "Okay, I'd better get home. I have to be back at five thirty. We try not to let the guests see us with our hands dirty."

I signaled the waiter for our check, having him charge it to our room. Then we stood from the table and before Kat even had her feet, Aria had pulled her into another hug. "God, it's good to see you."

"You too." Katherine squeezed her, then let go.

"What are you up to tomorrow?" Aria asked as we weaved past tables, making our way toward the exit.

"Not much," Kat answered.

"I need to get some work done first thing in the morning but come and find me whenever you get up. Just tell the front desk to page me."

"Okay." Kat hugged Aria again, then waved goodbye as her friend walked through the lobby. Katherine stared at her until she disappeared behind a door marked *Employees Only*, her shoulders sagging as it closed.

"You okay?"

"I wish I hadn't lost touch with her. With all of them."

"You found her now. And you'll always have Gemma close."

Katherine hummed. Was that a yes? A no? I used to understand her hums.

"Should we go up?" My mouth went dry as I finished the question. There would be no more escaping the bed or the fact that what I really wanted to do was kiss her again. To worship her body until we both passed out.

"Actually, I think I'm going to take a walk." Kat tucked a lock of hair behind her ear. "I'll be up in a while."

"Mind if I join you?"

"I was going to go to the beach. I thought you didn't like the smell."

Was that why it had taken her so long to get that stamp for Grandma's postcard earlier? Kat had probably escaped to the beach.

"The beach is fine." Not as good as Montana, but it was a sight to behold. My irritation earlier hadn't been with the smell but with how Kat had seemed to instantly fall in love with the place. "Lead the way."

She crossed the lobby and the moment we walked outside, the evening breeze picked up the loose curls of her hair. She'd spent an hour twisting it into soft waves, a style I'd seen more times on this trip than I had in the past five years combined.

My God, she was sexy. The clothes. Her hair. The dark, smoky shadow on her eyelids and the peach on her cheeks. My attention was so fixed on her that I barely registered the stairs as we descended the long staircase off the deck and I tripped over a few, catching myself on the railing before I fell. The steps led us down the cliffs to the beach below and though there was much to see, my eyes were glued to the sway of her hips and the way her hair swung across her shoulders.

Finally, when we hit the sand, I looked out and let the power of the ocean hit me square in the chest. It really was magnificent, like Kat. When I stopped fighting it, when I pulled the blinders down, it was spectacular.

Our feet dug into the beach as we made our way across the sand. Then we stood at the edge of the surf, staring out at the dark water, its waves catching the silver moonlight in diamond glitters.

"I like the beach," she whispered, so quietly I wasn't sure she was talking to me or simply telling herself.

"I didn't know you had a cat at the junkyard."

"It was only a stray but I loved it. I named her Patch. She was my companion. Londyn and Gemma were always the closest. Londyn dated Karson so the three of them were together a lot. And Aria and Clara were inseparable. I was normally the odd one out and that cat . . ."

That cat had been hers and hers alone. "Why didn't you bring Patch to Montana?"

"A wild cat on a bus?" She scoffed. "Yeah, that would have gone over well."

"Do you want to get a new cat?" We had a ton of barn cats roaming around free because they kept the mice away. There were constantly litters of kittens. Or I'd take her to a pet store and get her one from there.

"Maybe someday." She shrugged. "When I get my own place."

"You know, you don't have to move."

"Yes, I do."

"No, you don't. Look"—I turned to face her, taking her shoulders in my arms so she had to turn and face me too

—"I know things are strange right now. I don't regret what happened, but I'm not going to lie and say it hasn't fucked with my head. You're my friend. My best friend."

"I know." She stepped out of my grip and wrapped her arms around herself, rubbing at the bare skin of her arms. "I'm cold. I think I'll go back inside."

Without another word, without acknowledgement that I was trying to muddle my way through this, she spun away and marched toward the staircase.

"Fuck." I let her go, watching until she was halfway up the stairs before turning to the water.

The waves crashed on the sand, then retreated into the dark depths of the ocean. If I reached down and gripped the edge, no matter how hard I pulled, the wave would slip away. It was that way when I was training a stubborn horse. The harder I tugged on the reins, the longer the fight, and inevitably, I'd lose.

Maybe I was pulling too hard on Kat. She'd asked to forget about the sex and pretend it hadn't happened. Maybe we should.

She could keep her secrets.

And I could keep mine.

I stayed on the sand until the moon was far above my head, then slowly made my way to our room. The lights were off when I eased the door open except for the lamp on my nightstand. I hurried through brushing my teeth and pulling on a pair of cotton pajama pants, then I eased under the fluffy comforter, savoring the feel of the cool cotton on my naked chest and back.

"Kat." I turned on my side, facing her. She had her back to me and had stuffed a pillow in the center of the bed. "You asleep?"

"Yes."

I grinned. "Can I ask you a question?"

"No."

I asked it anyway. "Why don't you want to go back to California?"

Tell me. Please, talk to me. I was pulling again, something I'd convinced myself on the beach I wouldn't do, but I was desperate. I craved information even more than her luscious body.

She shifted, inching farther away and burrowing deeper under the covers. We didn't need the pillow between us. She was already miles and miles away. "Good night, Cash."

CHAPTER TEN

KATHERINE

"When I said come and find me in the morning, I didn't expect you to get up this early." Aria dragged a long hose across the deck of The Gallaway, moving down the row of potted flowers.

I tugged the hose, giving it slack. "I was up."

After next to no sleep last night, I'd snuck out of the hotel room while Cash had snored quietly into his down pillow. Before dawn, his arm had crept over the divider I'd placed in the center of the mattress and when his hand had rested on my hip, I'd slid from the sheets and tiptoed my way out of that bedroom.

It was supposed to be a dream, sleeping side by side with Cash. Except in the dream, he cuddled me in his arms as I drifted off to sleep. There was no need for his and her sides of the bed. We'd wake together in the morning to share a kiss. The stark gap between the fantasy and reality had sent me scurrying to the lobby this morning after dressing in the dark bathroom and tying my hair into a knot.

I'd been on one of the cushioned benches in the lobby, waiting for the espresso bar to open, when Aria had arrived promptly at five thirty. She'd let me tag along with her as she'd worked.

We'd been watering flowers for the past hour. Before that, I'd carried a garbage bag behind her, following as she pruned flower beds and deadheaded hanging baskets.

At least someone wanted my help. I'd checked for emails and texts and missed calls from Montana and to my increasing disappointment, there'd been none.

I shouldn't be so annoyed that things were running smoothly at the resort. That was what I'd worked for, right? Maybe if this vacation hadn't gotten so tragically off course, I would have enjoyed the break. But right now, I needed to feel useful. I needed the constant of work, something familiar to focus on when everything else was upside down.

Gardening with Aria had been a salvation.

The sun was up and the sky was more white than blue. The sound of the ocean was a constant calm in the background.

"What's up with you and Cash?" she asked as we walked down the deck.

"I'm surprised you waited this long to ask."

She laughed. "It's been killing me. Spill. That man is hot. Mega hot. So why are you *best friends?*"

"And coworkers."

She clicked her tongue. "And roommates."

"It's complicated." I groaned.

"Sleeping with your best friend tends to complicate things."

I blinked. "How did you know we were sleeping together?"

"Please." She rolled her eyes. "I was at the dinner table last night. Best friends who aren't having sex don't emit that kind of sexual tension."

I groaned again, my shoulders slumping. "It just happened on this trip. It was the first time and . . . ugh."

"Please don't tell me that man is bad in bed. It'll break my heart."

"No. Definitely not bad." The memory of his hands running over my skin, the way his mouth was hot and wet and so fucking talented, made me shiver. And that beard. That goddamn beard. My cheeks heated. "Really, really *not bad.*"

Cash had probably ruined me for any other man.

"Then tell me why you are down here with me this morning, schlepping around the hotel, doing gardening work, while that sexy cowboy is in a bed upstairs."

"He's my best friend." I sighed. "Or he was my best friend. Now . . . I don't know. Everything is different. It's like we don't know how to be around one another."

"Got it. You want to stay friends and he doesn't."

I twirled a finger in the air. "Other way around."

"Oh." She straightened, letting the water run on the deck boards. "You're in love with him."

"I'm in love with him," I whispered. Had I ever let those words escape my lips? "I don't think I've ever admitted that out loud."

Aria took a step closer and put her hand on my shoulder. "He doesn't feel the same."

"No. I'm firmly in the friend zone. He calls me Kat, like the cute little sister he never had."

"But you slept together."

"I don't understand it either." Because Cash had been the one to make the move. He'd come to my room and kissed me. Why? Was it because I'd been the only woman in the vicinity? Had it been an experiment? "He says he doesn't want to pretend it didn't happen, but I think that was just because he's trying to save my pride."

When we got home, I doubted he'd be forthcoming about what had really happened on this trip. I didn't want to tell his family anyway. It was far too humiliating since Carol, Gemma and, I suspected, Liddy knew I was in love with him.

If they found out we'd had sex but were definitely *not* together, all I'd earn was pity.

I hated pity.

"I can't keep doing this anymore."

"Have you told him how you feel?" Aria asked.

"No. I'm a coward."

"Or maybe you're protecting your heart. There's no shame in that."

Self-preservation was something I'd learned early on. It had taken me a long time to break the habits from my childhood. I shut down and shut people out when I didn't feel safe. There was no question that Cash cared for me and wanted to protect me. But that didn't mean I was safe with him.

It wasn't just my heart, my love life, on the line. If I lost Cash, I'd lose his family too.

He would always be a Greer.

And I was the hired help.

"Maybe if it was just us, I would have told him," I said. *Maybe not.* "But with his family involved, it gets messy. I couldn't have asked for a better home. They took me in and have taught me so much. They gave me a trade and work experience. I truly love them and I don't want to lose them."

"Do you really think they'll kick you out on the street if you and Cash aren't friends?"

"No. They'll support me no matter what happens with Cash. They're amazing people. But if I admit to Cash that I have feelings for him and he rejects them, I won't put myself through the misery of reliving that at the family dinner each week. Things will be awkward, whether we pretend or not. And he's their son."

The Greers would never kick me out on the street but

Carol and the ten-thousand-dollar check in my purse sure had opened the door for me to leave on my own volition.

"Maybe he won't reject you."

I scoffed. "We had sex two nights ago. He can barely talk to me or touch me. Cash is a good man and won't admit that he regrets it. But I know him very, very well. He regrets it. The rejection is coming. He's just working through his mind how to deliver it gently."

"Ouch." Aria winced. "Sorry."

"Me too."

Maybe we'd recover from this trip. If I didn't admit out loud that I loved him, he'd never know the truth and we could move forward like this was nothing more than a slipup by two people on vacation.

I tugged on the hose, pulling it toward the next planter, ready to get back to work. There was something soothing about being productive, not dwelling on the mistakes I couldn't correct.

"Do you think you could go back to being friends?" Aria asked as we shuffled along.

"I don't know."

When I looked back over the past decade, there hadn't been a time when I hadn't loved Cash. First as friends, then more. It was that slow build, like the growth of an evergreen. Or the rising tide. One minute, you looked down and saw a huge expanse of sand. The next, the water was crashing at your feet.

I glanced over my shoulder to the view. There was

nothing tropical about Heron Beach. There were no cabanas on the sand. No women in skimpy bikinis and floppy hats drinking cocktails with pink umbrellas.

Still, it was a beautiful change of scenery from the majestic and rugged Montana landscape. It was every bit as daunting, with the water stretching farther than the eye could see, but stunning nonetheless. It was impossible not to stare and count my heartbeats against the rhythm of the waves.

The Oregon coast was brutally breathtaking. Large, black rocks stood proud off the shores. Bold structures that had refused to succumb to the ocean's power. Their magnificence contrasted with the sandy shores, smooth and pristine. There was peace in the sand's submission.

Maybe it was time for me to surrender too.

Aria sprayed the last bloom of flowers and we returned to the spigot, turning off the water and coiling the hose away. She dried her hands on her jeans. I wasn't sure how she could wear a white hotel T-shirt and not get it smudged with dirt, but it was spotless, as was the monogrammed G on the breast pocket.

"What's next?" *Please don't tell me to go away.* If I didn't have something to do, I might be tempted to return to the room.

"I forgot this book I promised one of the girls I'd lend her so I was going to run home and grab it. Want to come?"

"Are you going to get sick of me tagging along with you all day?"

Aria surprised me by pulling me into a tight, short hug. Then she released me and nodded to the sidewalk that wrapped around the building. "Let's go."

"I don't remember you being such a hugger," I teased.

"That's Clara's fault. We always hugged goodbye and hello. Now that we don't live together, I find myself hugging everybody else to compensate."

I fell into step beside her as she walked away from the hotel. It was early so the sidewalks weren't yet crowded with people. I waited for her to stop at one of the cars parked beside us, but she kept on walking, leading us away from the beach and into a neighborhood. In a town this size, I guess walking was probably the quickest way to work.

"I feel bad for not asking more about Clara last night. How is she?" I asked.

"Good. She lives in Arizona with her son, August."

"I didn't realize she had a son."

Aria nodded. "He's four. Smartest kid I've ever met in my life. He loves his Aunt Aria almost as much as he loves his mom."

"And his dad?"

She shook her head. "Not in the picture. Clara cut him loose when Gus was a baby. She knew he was never going to be a good father, so rather than try unsuccessfully to turn him into one, she had him sign over his rights and moved away from Vegas so he wouldn't be close."

"Do you see them often?"

"Every couple of months. In the summer, they come to see me because I'm so busy and Arizona is hot. In the winter, I fly down a few times. Thanksgiving. Christmas. Mostly, I try to plan my trips around Clara's boss's schedule. I hate him with the fire of a thousand suns, so I make sure he's gone when I visit."

"What's the deal with her boss?" I asked.

"He's this rich, smug guy." Her lip curled. "Clara worked for him in Vegas as his assistant. When he decided to move to Arizona, he offered to take her along. The timing worked out because it was after Gus was born and she wanted to get out of Vegas anyway. So he bought her a car and built a guest house on his property so she wouldn't have to find an apartment."

"Okay," I drawled. "That sounds . . . nice? What am I missing?"

"Ugh. Not you too. Clara defends him mercilessly. She's always telling me that he's a good man. That he's kind to August and pays her more than she'll ever make at another job. But he grates on my every nerve. He throws money around like it's meaningless. He's spoiled. He likes to remind me that I'm the lesser fraternal twin." Aria's hands balled into fists. "We've learned to avoid one another so that Clara isn't in the middle."

We changed directions, starting up a side street and

making our way farther and farther from The Gallaway. Aria set a fast pace, one that made it hard for me to study the neighborhood, but that didn't stop me from trying. My eyes darted everywhere, taking in the green lawns and blooming trees. The homes were painted in light colors from baby blue to sage green.

For a woman who hadn't traveled much in her life, it was invigorating to experience something new. Heron Beach screamed casual. Welcoming. Friendly.

I loved Montana.

But I could love Oregon too.

"I like it here," I confessed as Aria made another turn on our way to her home.

"Me too. I drew the lucky straw when I found my job at The Gallaway."

"I feel the same about finding the Greers."

Regardless of the mess I'd made in my relationship with Cash, I loved the resort. But maybe my job there was done. Maybe it was time to take on a new challenge. Leaving Montana would be excruciating, especially now that Gemma was there, but soon, she'd have a baby.

Soon, her last name would be Greer.

I would always be a Gates.

Aria pointed to a row of two-story condos ahead on the street. "That's my place."

I didn't have to ask which of the four front doors was hers. The hotel had stunning flower displays and her home was no different.

A purple and pink fuchsia hung from the porch beam. I counted ten planters, all of varying sizes and colors and shapes, staged beside the front door. The sweet floral scents filled the air and I took a long inhale as Aria unlocked her door.

I should have suspected more of the same inside.

"This is beautiful." My wide eyes scanned the interior as Aria led me through the short entryway and into her living room.

She'd created a beach cottage with white sheer curtains, cozy cream furniture and lush greenery. This was a cookie cutter condominium complex but she'd turned her condo into something unique.

After the way her and Clara's parents had died, I was glad that she'd found some serenity. In a way, this reminded me of their delivery truck in the junkyard. While I'd painted the inside of my tent with bright colors, a meadow and flowers, Aria and Clara's home had always been bright. Even in what was essentially a steel truck, they'd found the light.

The delivery truck had been in an accident, hence the reason it was at a junkyard. They'd turned the jagged holes in the walls and ceiling into windows. Aria had filled the place with plants and Clara had added her own gentle touch with tidy bedrolls and shelves made out of tattered books.

Aria walked to the coffee table, something made from a piece of driftwood, and plucked up a paperback. "This is my book club's favorite reread."

"I love that you're in a book club."

Aria laughed. "This is a small town. Us locals stick together. Things get hectic during tourist season, but in the winter, when it's cold and gray, we sort of band together to keep from going crazy."

"We do the same in Montana. We still have guests in the winter so it's not like there isn't a peak season for us with skiing and snowmobiling. But it's slower than the summer months. And when we get a big snow, we'll find ourselves in someone's house, eating and playing games and reading and sitting around a fire."

"I meant what I said last night. I'm going to have to come and visit you and see this place for myself."

I smiled but stayed quiet. Would I still be there?

Aria and I didn't linger in her home. We returned on the same path that we'd taken, giving me a second taste of the allure and charisma of the locals' Heron Beach. When The Gallaway came into view and the bustle of downtown began to crowd the sidewalks, I took one last glance over my shoulder to the quieter streets behind.

The sound of the ocean in the distance filled my ears. The laughter and smiles from the guests coming and going from the hotel were contagious. When we walked into the lobby, the line at the espresso counter was ten deep but no one seemed to mind having to wait for their latte. The restaurant where we'd had dinner last night was closed, but the café next door was crowded for breakfast.

Was my crush on The Gallaway because I was on vacation? Because I was off duty? I could enjoy the bustle of the guests and not worry about their enjoyment. Customer satisfaction was the last thing on my mind.

"Aria, there you are." The same suited gentleman I'd seen her with yesterday appeared at our sides.

"Hey, Mark. What's up?"

"Whenever you're free, would you mind stopping by my office?"

"Sure. I'd like you to meet someone. Katherine Gates, this is Mark Gallaway. My boss."

"Nice to meet you." My heart did a little lurch as I held out my hand to shake his. Gallaway. As in The Gallaway?

"Katherine and I are old friends," Aria said. "We grew up in the same town. Now she runs a fancy guest ranch in Montana."

"Ah. Are you staying here at the hotel?"

"I am. It's lovely."

"We're proud of it." He grinned. "The Gallaway has been in my family for three generations."

Mark Gallaway was likely in his late forties. There were streaks of gray in his brown hair and fine lines around his eyes. But with that suit and his tall stature, he looked every bit the millionaire I suspected he was. I knew how much a hotel like this could potentially rake in, especially if run well.

"What's the name of your resort in Montana?" he asked.

"The Greer Ranch and Mountain Resort."

His eyes widened. "No kidding?"

"Have you heard of it?" Aria asked him.

"Often." He nodded. "I stayed there about five years ago. I was with a group of guys who went in the fall to go hunting. It's one of a kind. World renowned."

A blush crept into my cheeks and I fought a smile. "Like you, we're proud of it too."

"It's not easy to get a reservation there these days. My friends and I have been talking about going back, but you're booked out for the next three years."

"Hunting season is popular, but occasionally we'll get a cancelation. I can add you to the wait list if you'd like."

"I was told there isn't a wait list."

I leaned in close, Mark mirroring me, and lowered my voice. "There is if you know the general manager."

He leaned back and burst out laughing. "You've made my day, Ms. Gates. How long have you been the GM?"

"Four years."

"Well, I commend you. My visit to Montana was one I'll never forget. In the most positive way."

"Thank you." I shared a smile with Aria. "I'll let you two get back to work. Call me later?"

She nodded. "Now that you've made my boss's day, I'll be taking the afternoon off. I'll find you when I'm done."

"Wait." Mark raised his hand, stopping me before I could leave. "I have to ask. And you should know that this is very unlike me. I realize it's not exactly the polite way to do business, attempting to recruit another establishment's employee."

My jaw nearly dropped. Was he going to offer me a job? I might have been toying with the idea of moving, but I wasn't ready to decide. My pulse raced and my fingers trembled as he reached into his suit jacket and pulled out a business card.

"My general manager is retiring in three months. Aria has pitched in to help ease the transition but she wants to be in management about as badly as I want to water the plants."

Aria hummed her agreement.

"I'm having a hell of a time finding an experienced replacement." Mark handed me his card. "If you're ever interested in a location change—"

"She's not."

My head whipped to the side as a familiar, towering figure crowded into the space between me and Aria.

"Cash Greer." He held out his hand to Mark.

Mark returned Cash's handshake, looking guilty for having just been busted *poaching*. "Mr. Greer. Welcome to The Gallaway. If there's anything I can do to improve your stay, please let me know."

Cash nodded and slipped his hand around my elbow. "Katherine, may I speak with you for a moment?"

Damn. He'd called me Katherine. I was not going to like this conversation.

"Sure." There was no point arguing. Cash was not going to leave me here with Mark. "It was a pleasure meeting you, Mr. Gallaway."

"Mark. Please." He gave me a slight bow, then backed away. "The pleasure was mine."

Aria followed him toward the front desk, mouthing, "Later."

I nodded and steeled my spine, then turned to face an angry—*extremely* angry—Cash Greer.

CHAPTER ELEVEN

KATHERINE

The door slammed behind Cash as we walked into our hotel room. He strode past the unmade bed to the windows, practically ripping them apart as he flung the drapes away from the glass.

He hadn't spoken a word on the elevator ride to the second floor, but the lecture and fight were coming. Cash didn't lose his composure often, which was why our arguing on this trip was so abnormal. When angry, he'd close down and disappear to spend some time on a horse until he'd had some time to cool off.

We were a long way from his horses.

I braced when he turned from the window and planted his fists on his hips.

"What *the fuck* was that?"

"Nothing." When his hazel eyes turned hard as stone,

I realized playing dumb had been the wrong decision. "I was just talking with Aria's boss."

"He offered you a job."

"Not officially," I muttered.

Mark Gallaway hadn't even seen my résumé. He might decide to find someone with broader experience when he learned that the only people I'd ever worked for were the Greers and that my education had peaked at a GED.

Cash huffed and shook his head. "You didn't turn him down."

"Please." I rolled my eyes. "He was joking, Cash."

"You didn't turn him down." He pinned me with that cold stare.

My feet were glued to the carpet and my heart raced. No, I hadn't turned Mark down. A week ago, I would have politely declined and returned the business card instead of tucking it into my jeans pocket as I walked to the elevator.

"It's flattering," I admitted. "And maybe a bit tempting."

At my confession, Cash's face turned to ice. There was no easy smirk or warm smile lurking beneath the surface. His eyes flashed with betrayal. He looked at me like I was a stranger.

I opened my mouth to say something, but what? I wouldn't apologize for speaking the truth.

His nostrils flared and the fury emitting from his broad shoulders slammed into me like a tidal wave. "Why?" he asked through gritted teeth, then pointed to the bed. "Because of this?"

Yes. No. Maybe. I struggled to articulate an answer, so I threw out some questions of my own instead. "Haven't you ever wanted something different? Haven't you ever wanted more?"

"More?" He scoffed. "We've given you everything."

"And I'm grateful but—"

"Are you? Because the fact that you didn't tell that son of a bitch no on the spot doesn't feel much like gratitude. It feels a lot like a slap in the face for everything my family has handed you."

My mouth fell open. "Excuse me? Don't you fucking dare make me out to be some charity case. I worked my ass off for your family. I *earned* what I've achieved. Me."

Through blood, sweat and tears. The last time I'd been a charity case had been in California, sitting on a hot curb, begging for spare change. I'd vowed then to take control of my life and never be a beggar again.

"But you want more," he shot back. An unspoken *selfish* hung in the air.

"I want . . . I don't know. Can't I at least explore my options?"

"For what? Are you going to move here and work for a fancy hotel that's focused on turnover, not experience?"

That had been my marketing line. When I'd taken over as the manager at the resort, I'd made sure all of the Greers knew that in order to take the place to the next level, our marketing pitch had to be in sync. We weren't selling a comfortable stay or plush hotel room. We were selling an experience.

For Cash to throw that in my face, I'd done my job well.

"I can't fucking believe this," he said before I could come up with something to say. Some of the fury vanished but the hurt in his voice intensified. "I can't believe you'd leave us. You're part of our family."

"No, I'm not."

He winced. "If you truly believe that, then I'm ashamed of us. Because you are. You are one of us."

Ouch. Cash's words were a slap across the face. But the guilt was what hurt the worst.

He wasn't wrong.

I did feel like part of their family—most of the time. Liddy brought me flowers from the grocery store when she saw a bundle I'd like. Carol always managed to find the best birthday gifts, even when I didn't know what I wanted. Jake and JR and Easton protected me. They doted on me but respected my opinion and position. They'd all treated me like a part of their family.

Was I really throwing them away? Why? So what if Cash didn't love me. So what if we'd had sex. Yes, it would be miserable to see him fall in love with another woman and get married someday. Yes, it would be painful to see him teach his children to ride a horse or throw a ball. Hard to witness, but not unlivable.

I guess I hadn't broken the habits of my childhood like I'd thought.

When the world got to be too much, when my heart and spirit were broken, I ran.

My chin quivered and I bit the inside of my cheek. But despite my best effort to thwart it, a tear dripped down my cheek.

"We never fight," he whispered. The shreds of Cash's anger vanished and he put a hand to his heart, clutching his chest like there was a wound beneath the skin. "What is happening to us?"

"I don't know," I lied.

I knew exactly what was happening to us.

We were coming to an end.

Cash and I would go home to Montana. I'd return to being an honorary member of the Greer family, working at the resort and living my life. But my friendship with Cash would never look the same.

This was the end.

"Talk to me." He crossed the room and put his hands on my shoulders.

There was nothing to say and if we only had a fraction of time left, I didn't want to spend it fighting.

I rose on my toes, letting my hands slide up his chest until my fingertips found their way into the longer strands of hair at the nape of his neck. I pulled him to me and brushed my lips against his.

Cash didn't hesitate. His arms banded around my

back, crushing me against his strong body, and he fused his lips to mine. Teeth nipped. Tongues tangled. Heartbeats thundered.

I yanked and pulled at Cash's shirt, working frantically to get the buttons undone. He reached between us and loosened his belt, letting it fall free as the scrape of his zipper sounded past the blood rushing in my ears.

With his jeans open, I reached beneath the elastic of his boxers, finding his swollen shaft and wrapping it in my fist. Cash groaned into my mouth, tearing his lips away from mine as I stroked his velvety flesh.

He dove under the hem of my tee, his calloused palms rough and hungry against my skin. Cash's hands were so large that they spanned the length of my ribs. He held me, immobile and panting, as he tore his lips away and leaned back.

The lust in his eyes was heady. Lust, for me. It was a cheap substitute for love, but my foolish heart didn't care.

"I don't have any more condoms," he warned.

I gripped his shaft hard, pulling him closer. I'd been on birth control for years. "I'm safe."

"So am I."

I stroked him again, this time adding a single nod.

Cash dragged his shirt off his body, then crowded me, his lips recapturing mine. His height forced me to bend backward, so far that if not for his firm hold, I would have dropped to the floor.

I clung to him, letting go of his throbbing cock to

clutch his shoulders as he swept me into his arms and walked us to the bed, not once breaking from my lips.

He set me on the mattress but before he could trap me underneath his body, I twisted, shifting to push his body into the soft sheets instead. Cash went willingly to his back, giving me a wicked grin as I straddled his waist and whipped my shirt off my torso. My fingers fumbled to unclasp my bra.

The pulse in my core ached, desperate for him to be inside. I worked the buttons of my jeans free, leaning forward to shimmy them and my lace panties off my hips while Cash shoved at his jeans and boxers. The moment the denim was on the floor, Cash's hands palmed my bare ass, kneading and working their way toward my wet center from behind.

I straddled Cash's waist, my hands sliding up the hard ridges of his stomach to the dusting of hair between his pecs.

His hands came up to cup my breasts. "Damn, you are gorgeous."

I covered his hands with mine, letting my head loll to the side and my eyes close as he squeezed, his thumbs toying with my pebbled nipples. His scent surrounded me, the cologne he'd put on this morning and his own natural, masculine spice.

Cash slipped one hand free and I let my own fingers pinch the nipple in his absence. I opened my eyes to take him in, and the hunger in his eyes, the desire, made me tremble.

He dragged a finger through my slippery folds, barely grazing my clit before bringing his finger to his mouth to lick my juices. "So sweet."

My core spasmed and I forgot about torturing my own nipple and reached between us, taking his cock in my hand at the same time I lined my entrance up with the tip and sank down.

"Oh God," I gasped, savoring the stretch and feel of his bare erection filling me. I spread my thighs wider, taking him as deeply as possible, rolling my hips to grind my clit against the hard root of his cock.

"Fuck, sweetheart, you feel so good." He arched his neck into the pillow, his Adam's apple bobbing as he swallowed and sucked in a jagged breath. Cash's hands came to my hips, picking me up like I weighed nothing, before dropping me back down, connecting us again.

I planted my hands on his chest and lifted myself and as I slammed down again, he thrust his hips upward, going so deep I gasped. The tip of his cock hit a spot inside that made me whimper. My hands went back to my breasts to tug at my nipples as we rocked into one another, up and down, until my legs trembled and I chased my release with reckless abandon.

"Ride me, Kat." His hands dug into the curves of my hips, the roped muscles in his forearms flexed tight.

Faster and faster, I rode him, just like he'd demanded.

My orgasm came without warning. I shattered, my entire body clenching as stars exploded in my eyes, blinding me from reality. I cried out, reveling in the best orgasm of my life and the feel of Cash's roaming hands as I pulsed around him, over and over and over.

I was still riding out the aftershocks when Cash flipped us in a swift spin. He dropped a soft kiss to the corner of my lips, then took my hands in his, lacing our fingers together at our sides.

This man was made to pleasure women. Hovering above me, his eyes darkened to caramel and hunter-green gems, he was unabashedly seductive. His body was a work of art and strength.

The roughhewn, captivating mountains of Montana, the dynamic, awe-inspiring beaches of Oregon. No matter where I traveled in this world, nothing would ever compete with the view of Cash in this moment.

Sunshine streamed through the window like it had the first time we'd been together, illuminating his features. I memorized the sound of his hitched breath. I studied the way his tongue darted out to lick his bottom lip every few strokes and the soft hum he gave me when I flicked his nipples, the sound sweeter than any song or symphony. I took a mental picture of the way he looked when his eyes drifted closed in ecstasy, his sooty eyelashes sable crescents against his tanned skin.

I savored every second, knowing that we were racing toward the harrowing end.

Cash's eyes locked with mine, the shaking in his body the only warning he gave before coming inside me in long, hot strokes. I didn't blink for fear of missing a second of the rapture that played across his face.

Spent from his release, Cash collapsed onto me, his body as limp as my own. When he'd regained his breath, he shifted to the side, releasing my hands and circling me in his arms, my back flush against his damp chest.

This was why our friendship was over.

I'd never be able to look at him again and not think about how perfectly we fit together. I'd never get a whiff of his cologne without remembering how it smelled mingled with mine.

Cash took a long inhale of my hair, holding me closer. "We should go home."

Except home wasn't the same anymore and I wasn't in a rush to face it.

He held me until the sweat from our bodies cooled and the growling of his stomach drove us apart. "I'm going to take a quick shower, then maybe we can get something to eat."

"Okay." I nodded as he kissed my temple. Then I pressed my nose into the pillow, taking one more moment to remember how he'd felt inside me.

The water in the bathroom turned on and I slid off the bed, my legs wobbly, and hurried to dress. Before Cash could stop me, I rushed from the room, easing the door closed as quietly as possible.

Leaving him so I could find a place to cry.

Alone.

———

"YOU RAN AWAY." Cash dropped to the beach to sit beside me. The strands of his hair were damp from the shower.

"Sorry," I said, my voice raspy with unshed tears.

I'd come out to the beach to cry but the moment I'd plopped down in the sand, I hadn't had the energy. Because my tears weren't going to make this any easier and at this point, I needed to save my strength.

Cash had been right earlier. It wasn't fair to abandon the Greers and take a spur-of-the-moment job offer. But I was going to move out of his house. I was going to stay in the staff quarters for a while. And I was going to start mapping out what my future looked like.

Without him as the constant of my universe.

"Did I do something?" he asked.

"No." I looked at his profile, melting at the concern in his voice. "I just needed some air. It's been a string of emotional days."

He huffed a laugh. "It's been less than a week since we left. Feels like longer."

"Yeah," I murmured, turning to the ocean.

There were families building sandcastles. Couples

taking selfies. Not a soul on the beach was without a smile, except for the two of us.

"Am I losing you?" he asked, his gaze straight ahead.

"I'll always be your friend." I leaned over, resting my head on his shoulder.

"That's not what I'm asking."

"I know," I whispered.

"Talk to me."

"I don't know what to say." *I love you?* No, thanks. My wall of self-preservation was about to double in thickness.

"Why don't you want to go to California?"

"Because there's nothing for me there but old memories. I'd rather focus on making new ones."

There was no family. No friends. I didn't want to see the junkyard, because I was worried that the reality of where we'd lived would be too much to take.

"Do you want to take a job here?" There was a twinge of pain in his voice, likely because he knew the answer.

"Maybe. I think . . . I think I'd like to stay in Heron Beach a while longer. With Aria."

Carol had been right all along. I needed to take some time, to think and decide.

Cash didn't have to be told he wasn't invited. He nodded, his jaw clamping shut. Then he stared at the water and the other tourists, the two of us sitting on the beach for hours.

"Do you remember the goat?" he asked as a dog ran by with a frisbee in its mouth.

"You meant the white devil that tried to kill me?"

He chuckled. "Dad asked me about a month ago if we should get some goats to graze."

I shuddered. "Tell me you told him no."

"I said, 'Over my dead body. Kat will smother me in my sleep if she finds out I agreed to raise goats.'"

I smiled. That was exactly what I would have threatened, verbatim.

Liddy was the one who'd brought a goat to the ranch. She'd seen a baby at the farm and ranch supply store in Missoula, and JR, being the loving, doting husband he was, had bought his wife a goat. Cash and Easton had built their mom a pen for the animal but somehow, that goat always managed to find its way out. Or its way over, we learned.

The damn thing could jump like Air Jordan.

It had never been a nice, sweet animal. To this day I believed the display goat that Liddy had seen was a fake. Because the goat she brought home loved nothing more than to chase unsuspecting humans and head butt them in the ass—specifically, me.

The goat hated me.

One day, I brought Liddy a pie I'd made from scratch. It had been one of my first since she'd taught me how to bake. She'd spent years teaching me little tricks and handing down her favorite recipes.

I was so damn proud of that strawberry rhubarb pie I

didn't want to wait. The second it was cool enough to carry without an oven mitt, I drove it over to her house.

Except I didn't realize the demon had escaped its pen.

I parked, took my pie and got out of my car, nudging the door closed with my hip. That fucking goat came around the corner of their house and I panicked, running into a field with it chasing behind.

Cash had been out riding that day. He caught sight of me and barreled toward us, chasing the goat off with his horse and swiping the pie dish out of my hand right before I tripped.

Maybe another man would have tried to save me from falling. Not Cash. He knew the hours I'd spent with Liddy in the kitchen. That was before we'd moved in together, but he knew how important it was for me to bake her a gift.

So I'd eaten a face full of dirt. But he'd saved my pie.

That day, I'd fallen in love with Cash. That day had been the turning point from like to love. That day was also the last day a goat had lived on the Greer ranch.

"Remember the time we went dancing at the bar and you bent to flip me over and your pants split down the ass?" I asked. "I've never laughed so hard in my life."

"In my defense, those were very old pants." He chuckled. "How about that time you and Easton got into an eating contest over a plate of nachos?"

"Please don't say that word." I grimaced. Nachos were now classified with green beans.

We talked for another hour, reminiscing about old times. It was what I'd miss as we adjusted to a new normal. I'd mourn the loss of our friendship for a long, long time.

My butt had fallen asleep. My legs needed to stretch. I opened my mouth to tell Cash I was going to take a walk down the beach when suddenly his hands were cupping my face and his tongue swept past my lips.

I moaned, falling into him as we kissed on the beach. The taste of his lips, the soft caress of his hands, the tickle of his beard, it was the best kiss of my life.

He shoved off the sand, holding out a hand to help me to my feet. Then he threaded my fingers through his and led me across the beach to the stairs that led to The Gallaway. We didn't pause or linger on the way to our room. We didn't hesitate to strip one another of our clothes and fall into bed, a tangled mess of limbs.

We passed the hours of the day exploring each other's bodies. When Aria called, I told her I would just see her tomorrow. Cash and I ordered room service and ate naked in bed. And only when the sunlight had faded to moonlight through the window did we settle in to sleep. And to speak.

"I don't think we should tell anyone about this," I said. We were facing each other, our hands joined between us. "When we get home."

He stared into my eyes and kissed one of my knuckles.

I waited, wondering what was going on in his head but he didn't speak. "Cash."

Silence.

"Say something," I whispered.

"Tomorrow." He tucked a strand of hair away from my face. Then he closed his eyes and drifted to sleep.

Tomorrow.

Tomorrow, he'd say his goodbye.

The morning sun was barely above the horizon when I snuck out of the hotel the next morning. Once again, I took the coward's way out. Because I couldn't say goodbye. Not yet.

So I left him a note.

See you in Montana.

CHAPTER TWELVE

CASH

"Could this elevator be any fucking slower?" I muttered. "I hate this hotel."

The couple standing beside me shared a look that I caught in the reflection from the polished silver walls.

I ignored them and growled. Was this how horses felt when you trapped them in their stalls? Itching and uncomfortable and desperate for freedom?

My molars ground together, the grating sound filling the car, until the light bar finally illuminated the number one. The doors slid open and though I wanted out, I waved a hand for the couple to exit first. They skittered away.

I marched from the elevator, scanning the lobby for Katherine. The note she'd left me this morning was crumpled so tight I could use it as a golf ball.

When my hand had stretched for hers this morning,

I'd found stiff paper and cold cotton sheets instead of warm skin, and I was goddamn tired of searching for her in this place.

She didn't do this at home. She didn't disappear the moment I looked away. I found her at the office more often than not, but that was for work. She'd never avoided me so much.

Had she?

There was no sign of Kat in the lobby so I walked to the deck. She wasn't standing against the railing or sitting in one of the seats. A few people were out this morning on the beach, but none with her petite frame and dark hair.

I turned and strode through the lobby, heading for the front desk to page Aria. It was too early for shops to be open downtown and my guess was Kat was with Aria again.

"Good morning, sir," the man behind the counter greeted as I approached. "What can I help you with?"

"I'm—" A flash of a familiar smile caught the corner of my eye and I changed direction, walking away from the man and across the lobby for the hotel's café.

There she was. My beautiful, infuriating best friend and lover was seated at a small table across from the motherfucker who'd offered her a job yesterday.

My bootsteps echoed on the marble floor as I stormed into the café, bypassing the hostess, who had the good sense to give me a wide berth.

Katherine was laughing, covering her mouth with a

napkin as she chewed. There was a half-eaten croissant on a plate beside a mug of black coffee.

Mark Gallaway was relaxed in his chair, his legs crossed. "I can't believe you've never seen that movie."

Katherine shook her head, dropping her napkin and opening her mouth to respond when she caught me from the corner of her eye. Her smile fell. "H-hey."

I didn't bother with pleasantries. "Let's go."

A flush crept up her cheeks as her eyes darted between Mark and me. "I'll meet you in the room soon."

"Let's. Go," I repeated, doing my best to hold my temper in check. It was rare that I got this mad, but goddamn this woman, she was pushing me to every edge on the emotional cliff this week. "Now."

Kat arched an eyebrow. "I'm busy now."

Mark stared at me with a smug grin on his face, not bothering to hide it as he sipped his own coffee.

I stood tall and crossed my arms over my chest. "We can talk in private or we can talk right here. Doesn't matter to me. But we are talking."

Katherine held my gaze, her eyes narrowing. She knew me well and she knew I sure as fuck wasn't bluffing. "Five minutes."

"I'll wait."

"Fine," she huffed, dismissing me with a glare as she put on a smile for Mark. It wasn't her real smile. It was the polite and placating one she used for guests. "I'm so sorry, Mark. Will you excuse me?"

"No problem." He smiled at her. "You have my card."

"Yes." She reached for her purse hanging from the back of her chair and retrieved her wallet.

Mark waved it off. "On me. Please. I've enjoyed talking with you this morning. I hope to hear from you again soon."

Oh, fuck this guy. I dug for my own wallet in my jeans pocket, taking a crisp one-hundred-dollar bill from the fold and slapping it on the table. Then I jerked my chin toward the door.

Kat gave Mark an awkward smile as she stood, but the second her gaze landed on me, it was full of fire and venom.

She took my elbow and shoved me away from the table. I'd worn a T-shirt today rather than my normal button-up and her fingernails dug into my skin. "You're a child."

"No, I'm fucking pissed." I ripped my arm free of her grip, then clasped her hand and marched us toward the elevator.

"It couldn't wait five minutes?"

"No."

The elevator was empty as she stepped inside, yanking her hand free from mine to punch the button for our floor. Then she crossed her arms over her chest and shook her head. "That was embarrassing, Cash."

"So was waking up alone after last night."

Hadn't that been special? Hadn't I treated her like the treasure she was? Hadn't I promised we'd talk tomorrow?

Damn it, I had a lot to say. The words clogged my throat, scratching and pleading to be set free. But this was not something I wanted to do in public.

An elevator was not the place to tell your best friend that you were in love with her.

I'd known it yesterday, sitting beside her on the beach. Maybe I'd known it the day I'd first seen her at the ranch all those years ago.

I was in love with Kat.

Any other woman and I probably would have blurted it out last night, but she wasn't any woman. This was Kat. And to say those words, to take this leap, was risking our friendship. And it was risking her happiness.

I was a Greer. I'd always be a Greer. And if this thing between us didn't work out, she'd lose more than a boyfriend. She'd lose a mother, a father. Grandparents and a brother. Her job. Her house.

If Katherine didn't want to explore this thing, I knew, deep down, that eventually she'd leave Montana.

Maybe she'd already made that decision.

Maybe she didn't feel the same way.

Maybe I was twelve years too late.

We needed to go home. We needed to get on familiar ground and talk this through. If she thought I was leaving without her, she was insane. No way I'd leave her with all the shit we'd gone through this week. No way I'd leave her with vultures like Mark Gallaway circling.

"Did he offer you a job again?" I asked.

"Yes."

Son of a bitch. "And?"

"And what? We had this conversation last night. I'm just exploring options. Not all of us are content to settle for the same old thing."

"Settle." I scoffed. Her claws were coming out. "That's what you think."

"Yes." The elevator dinged and she flew past me, stomping down the hallway in her flip-flops to the room. She slid the key into the slot and turned the handle. I planted my hand in the door, pushing it with too much force. It slammed against the rubber stop with a bang before slamming closed behind me as I followed her into the room.

She was ready for the face-off. She stood in front of the TV with her arms crossed. My heart jumped into my throat. When Kat entered a battle, she usually walked away the victor.

Not this time. I wanted us both to win.

"I love my job," I said. Before we covered anything else, I wanted to clear the air. "All I've ever wanted to do was be a cowboy. That's not me settling, that's me understanding reality. I'm the second son, Kat. My entire life, my father has been grooming Easton to take over the ranch. And I'm okay with that. I don't need to be in charge everywhere because when I am in charge, they respect that. When one of them needs help with a horse, they come to me. The rest . . . it was never meant for me."

"Doesn't that bother you?"

"No." I sighed. "Why does it bother you?"

"Because it's not fair." She threw her hands in the air. "You deserve all of it. You deserve the chance to choose the job you want."

I really did love her. She was standing here, furious on my behalf, when there wasn't anything to be furious about. I stepped closer. "I did choose. I am exactly where I want to be in my life. I don't want or need it to change."

A flash of pain crossed her gaze. "Right. Well, I don't feel the same. Mark—"

"Screw Mark." My rage returned with a vengeance at his name. I spun around and walked to the closet, yanking out her suitcase. Then I brought it back and threw it on the bed. "Pack. We're going home."

This trip was a disaster and though I wanted to talk to Kat about the future, I sure as hell wasn't doing it when we were at each other's throats.

"I'm not ready to leave." She jutted out her chin.

"We're leaving."

"I don't take orders from you, Cash."

"Yeah? That's not how it went last night." I'd ordered her to come and she'd done it on my command.

Her lip curled. "You're an asshole."

"Maybe. But I'm not the one turning away from their

family without giving them a fighting chance. They deserve an explanation. If you leave like this, if you just don't come back, it will crush them. Grandma. Gemma. Mom. My mother loves you like her own."

"But I'm not her own!" Katherine's shout made me flinch. "She's not my mother. And do you know how painful it is to wish so badly it were true? To wish I could claim her?"

"No." I threw my arms in the air. "Because you don't talk to me. I've learned more about your past on this trip than I have in twelve years. Why?"

"I don't like to talk about my childhood."

"Even with me?" I pointed to my chest.

"Especially with you."

Fuck. Her words slashed me to the core. If she didn't trust me with her past, there was no way she'd trust me with the future.

"If you want to stay, then stay." I turned from her and strode for the door. I'd take a page from her playbook this morning and hit the beach to think. Get some air. Then I was finding an airport and getting the hell back to Montana where I belonged.

My hand gripped the door's handle just as a pair of dainty fingers touched my elbow.

"It's dirty," she whispered to my back. "It's grimy. And I hate the idea that you, of all people, might see me differently."

I turned and stared down at Kat. Her gaze was on the

floor so I hooked my finger under her chin and tipped it up until I got those blue eyes. "No matter what you say, no matter where you came from, you'll always be my Kat."

Her eyes turned glassy.

The sight of unshed tears, the struggle in her eyes was nearly too much to take. I wrapped my arms around her. "Talk to me. Please. I want to understand."

"It hurts."

"Because you're keeping it all inside. This isn't a burden you have to carry alone." I didn't care that I already knew the truth. I just wanted her to confide in me. To trust me.

And maybe once she did, I'd tell her my secret. We'd rip the past wide open so that we actually had a chance to start fresh.

Katherine nodded against my chest, then stepped free, retreating to the bed. She plopped on the end, her short legs dangling above the carpet.

I sat by her side, taking her hand in mine and lacing our fingers together.

"My mother was tall," she said. "When I was a little girl, I used to look up at her and wonder if I'd be tall too. I was tiny, always the short kid in school. They'd put me in the front row in every class photo because the other kids stood head and shoulders above me. I hated it. I just wanted to be tall."

"Like your mom." When I was a kid, I'd wanted to be strong like my dad.

"No, not like my mom. I didn't want to be like my mom. I just wanted to be tall."

Kat sat motionless, unblinking as she stared at the floor. The air conditioner kicked on, but it did nothing to suppress the thick air.

"The tall kids didn't get picked on," Kat said finally. "Their mothers didn't call them Runt. I was five when I learned that my name was Katherine. Five. She had to enroll me in school and when she told the secretary my full name, I remember thinking, *Who is Katherine Gates?* Until then, I'd always thought my name was Runt. That's what she called me. That's how she introduced me to others."

"What the fuck?" I stared down at her, my mouth hanging open. "She didn't call you by your name?"

Kat shook her head. "No."

"Had she meant it like . . . an endearment?"

"No."

My stomach clenched. How could a mother name her child and then not use that name?

"She didn't want me. To this day, I don't know why she kept me. Maybe to be her punching bag."

My heart stopped. "She hit you?"

"Pinched. Slapped. The occasional kick. I think my life would have been easier if I bruised easily."

"But you've got the toughest skin on the planet."

How many times had I teased her about it? The woman would run her shins into the coffee table and other than a slight red mark immediately afterward, she didn't bruise. The only time I'd seen her black and blue was when we'd been playing baseball for fun and she'd caught a ball with her eye instead of her hand. Even then, it had healed in a couple of days without a trace.

"What about your father?" Kat hadn't spoken of him, though I'd known she'd run away from her mother's home.

"I don't know who he is. Probably one of my mother's meth-head friends."

"Meth."

Kat nodded. "Mom's drug of choice during my teenage years. I didn't care because when she was using, she'd disappear for days on end. It was when she'd come home that things were bad."

"I don't . . ." Christ, I wanted to hold her. "I'm sorry."

"We never had money. If not for school food, I would have starved. She spent everything. Stole whatever I managed to scrape together, no matter where I hid it."

Which had led her to the sidewalk, where she'd sat and begged for money to buy some fucking shoes. My insides twisted into a knot. I *hated* this for her. I hated that she'd had to endure so much strife.

"After I met Karson and followed him to the junkyard, I went home. There were some kids at my high school in foster care and I didn't want to go through that, bouncing from place to place. The junkyard sounded fun so I spent a week slowly packing. Trying to make it inconspicuous. Then I waited for Mom to disappear. It took a week, but she left and I was ready. I figured I'd be long gone by the time she showed up again. But she only left for an hour. She came home and caught me three steps away from the door, carrying a garbage bag and a backpack." Kat's hand drifted to her eyebrow, to the small scar barely visible between the dark hairs.

I'd asked her once how she'd gotten that scar. "You didn't get that from running into a shelf, did you?"

"It was a shelf. I didn't run into it though. She pushed me and I fell. For a woman who constantly spoke about getting rid of me, she really hadn't liked that I was leaving. She flew into a rage and locked me inside my room. The window in my bedroom had been boarded up for years. I couldn't get the door open. She locked me up and left for a week. If not for the bottles of water and the loaf of bread that I'd already put in that backpack to take with me to the junkyard, I would have probably died."

"Kat—"

"I had to pee in the corner of my closet." Her jaw tensed, her eyes narrowing. "I hope it smelled for years after I left. I hope she had one sober day when she realized what she put me through."

I gulped. "How'd you get out?"

"One of her drug dealers came over because she owed him money. He opened my door, thinking she was locked inside. He took one look at me and decided I'd be payment enough."

"No." My stomach pitched. "He didn't—"

"I was so weak. So hungry. I wouldn't have been able to fight him off. But he got close enough, smelled the urine and decided a punch to the face was good enough. I blacked out and when I woke up, he was gone. He'd left the door open so I cleaned myself up, grabbed my bag of clothes and left. You know the rest."

"Kat, I'm sorry." My voice was hard to use past the lump in my throat. I clutched her hand to my heart and dropped a kiss to her knuckles. "I'm so, so sorry."

"It's okay," she whispered. There was a numbness to her voice. A robotic tone that I hadn't heard before. "I found my way out."

For a lot of years, I'd felt guilty about what I'd done to her mother. Maybe Kat would hate me for keeping this secret, but knowing this, how her mother had treated her . . .

The guilt was gone.

"Thank you for telling me." I clutched her hand, binding her to me so she couldn't flee. "Now I have to tell you something."

"About what?"

I met her blue eyes. "About your mother."

197

CHAPTER THIRTEEN

CASH

"What about my mother?" Kat slipped her hand free from my grasp.

Where did I even start? *Shit.* There was a reason I hadn't told her about this. A reason that I hadn't told anyone in my family.

Guilt.

I'd made a choice to protect Kat, and at the time, I'd been confident in my decision. I'd done it with her best interests at heart. But year after year, doubts had crept in, making me question my actions on that day. I realized now that I'd stayed quiet not to protect Kat, but to protect myself. I didn't want to lose her.

I hadn't wanted to miss this chance to love her and the chance she might love me back.

Fuck, this was going to be bad. She was going to hate me for this. Hell, I kind of hated myself.

"Cash," she warned.

"She came to the ranch," I admitted. "Your mother."

"What? When?"

"Five years ago." I remembered because it was the first weekend after Kat had moved into my place—our place. I'd wanted to give Kat the chance to settle in without feeling like I was hovering, so I'd left her alone on a Sunday and gone to work.

I was in the stables, in the arena halter-breaking a colt, when a woman appeared at the fence. One look and I knew she wasn't a guest. Her clothes were nice—jeans and a pink blouse. No-brand tennis shoes. Inexpensive clothing, not something any of our guests would have worn. And she was missing four front teeth.

Like Kat said, she was tall. I went over to the fence and she stood only a few inches shorter than my six foot two. She had Kat's hair, dark though streaked with thick strands of gray. Her eyes were blue but not as crystal clear as Kat's.

The resemblance didn't register until she asked to see her daughter, Katherine Gates.

"Five years?" Kat shook her head. "Why didn't you tell me?"

"She introduced herself. She told me her name was Jessica Gates and she was looking for her daughter, Katherine." Her visit had instantly put me on guard. Rightly so. "I asked what she wanted." I hadn't been nice about it. I think my exact words had been, *What the fuck do you want?* "She said that she needed to find you. To talk to you. I told her no."

"You what?" Kat shot off the bed, standing above me.

"I was trying to protect you. All I knew was that you'd run away from home. That you'd lived in a junkyard. You didn't speak of your parents but it didn't take much to put together that she wasn't a good mother. All of us had talked about it."

"You talked about me?" The color drained from her face. "Behind my back? Like a pity party."

"No, it wasn't like that. It was just . . . your story was shocking. None of us really knew what to think."

"So yes, a pity party. That's why you started inviting me to Friday night family dinners."

"No. Look, it wasn't like that. We just wanted to include you. Make sure you felt like you had a home. Is that so wrong?" And of all the staffers who'd come and gone at the ranch, none had ever fit into our circle like Kat.

"My mother." Kat crossed her arms over her chest. "What did she say?"

"When I told her no, she begged to see you." Jessica Gates had reached her bony fingers across the fence separating us as we'd spoken and grabbed my hand, squeezing it with more strength than I'd expected from a woman who looked like she'd lived hard.

"And you still turned her away. How could you?"

"Because she just wanted money." The hurt that flashed across Kat's face broke my heart. "I told her that we knew all about your childhood. That you were better off without her. And I told her that you didn't want to see her."

"You had no right."

"I was trying to protect you. I wanted to see what she'd do. How honest she was in her intentions. You know what it looks like when you roll onto the property." Like money. The lodge was enormous. The stables and barn too. The Greer Ranch and Mountain Resort was designed to impress the wealthiest people in the world.

"And?" Kat stared at me, her face twisted in rage, but the hurt was beginning to show through. Her features were beginning to crumple. Because she already knew where this was going.

"I told her I'd give her five thousand dollars, cash, to leave the ranch and leave you in peace."

She swallowed hard. "She took it?"

"Yes."

To her credit, Jessica had waged an internal debate. She'd stood across from me, her eyes cast to the dirt, and weighed my offer for a solid five minutes. As the time dragged on, I almost gave in. I almost offered to go get Kat and bring her to the lodge. But right before I could cave, Jessica held out her hand.

Maybe she thought that my five thousand dollars was more than she'd ever get from Kat. When the selfish bitch accepted my offer, I didn't waste a second before getting her off my ranch.

"She'd flown to Missoula, then paid for an Uber to drive her to the ranch. I went to the lodge. Got some money out of the safe in Dad's office. Then I gave it to her and drove her to the airport in Missoula myself."

The forty-mile trip was the longest of my life. A few times I caught Jessica catching a tear with her fingertips as she stared out the passenger window. When I pulled up to the airport's terminal, she opened the door, ready to leave without a word, but paused.

Tell her I'm sorry.

Then she was gone.

I'd wondered for the past five years if we'd see her again. If she'd come begging for more money now that she knew a trip to Montana was an easy payday. But I'd never seen Jessica again.

And for years, I'd unsuccessfully prodded Kat for information about her youth. I'd needed to know that I'd done the right thing by sending Jessica away.

"Did she ask about me?"

Damn it, this was going to hurt. "No."

Jessica hadn't once asked if her daughter was happy or safe or loved.

Kat dropped her gaze to the floor. Her hair draped in front of her face but I still saw the quiver of her chin.

"I'm sorry."

"You should have told me," she whispered.

"I know."

"How could you keep this from me? All these years?"

She looked up and the pain in her expression wasn't just from her mother's visit, but because I'd betrayed her.

"It was for your own good."

"Oh, fuck you," she snapped.

I flinched. "Kat—"

"You and your family are always trying to protect me. Except what any of you don't seem to realize is that I don't need your protection. Carol forbids me from touching base with the resort staff while I'm on this trip and it's for my own good. Gemma sets up this entire trip and it's for my own good. You don't tell me about my mother coming to find me ten years after I've seen her and it's for my own good. I don't need your protection. I'm capable of judging what's *for my own fucking good.*"

"We're just looking out."

"I don't need anyone to look out for me."

"That's what family does."

"Family?" She scoffed. "You sent my only living relative away. You took away the last chance I ever had to see my mother."

"I'm sorry. If it means that much, we can go find her. I'll go with you to California. We can leave today."

"Too late." Kat's eyes turned glacial and her expression flattened. "She's dead."

The air in the room went still. My heart dropped. "What?"

"She died of an overdose. Five years ago."

No. Oh shit, no.

"I remember because it was the second weekend after I moved in with you. We were supposed to have everyone over for pizza."

But she'd canceled because of a migraine. We'd rescheduled to another weekend. Except Kat didn't get migraines, did she? That was the one and only time I recalled her having one, and at the time, I hadn't realized it was a lie.

"How?" I choked out. How had she died? How had Kat known?

"The sheriff came out that morning. I was at the lodge, weeding one of the flower beds. I'd thought he'd come to have coffee with your dad. Instead, he'd come to find me. To tell me that my mother had been found dead in her home two days prior."

I stood, ready to hold her and tell her I was sorry, but she shook her head and took a step away. My feet froze.

"When her neighbor went through her things, she told me she found four thousand dollars cash in her purse. I never understood how, but now I know. The other thousand must have gone toward a plane ticket and however much it cost to flood her system with meth."

Fuck me. My head spun and I sank down to the edge of the bed. I'd given Jessica the money she'd used to end her life. Horror coursed through my system. Despair and guilt clouded my vision. I dropped my head forward, my elbows on my knees. "Kat, I'm sorry."

"She was clean before that. She'd changed her life."

"What?" My head snapped up. "How do you know?"

"Gemma's not the only one who can hire an investigator," she said. "After I found out she'd died, I had to settle her estate. Not that there was much. And I wanted to know what her life had been like but I didn't want to visit."

So she'd hired an investigator. Meanwhile the rest of us hadn't had a clue that she'd been carrying this burden alone.

Kat barked a mocking laugh. "Turns out, all she'd needed to get clean was for her daughter to abandon her. According to her records, she went to rehab about a year after I ran away from home. She stayed sober ever since. She worked at a local women's shelter. She moved into a nicer neighborhood. One of her coworkers at the shelter told my investigator that Mom had spent years setting aside money to go to Montana. She'd just been too scared to make the trip."

And I'd chased Jessica away.

I'd chased her back into the drugs that had cost her a daughter.

I'd chased her into a grave.

"I had her cremated and spread her ashes on Hangman Peak," Kat whispered.

"You did?" Hangman Peak was one of the hardest hikes we offered to our guests, but the view at the top was worth every step. I made it a point to go up there at least twice a year.

She lifted a shoulder. "I thought she would have liked the view."

"You went alone?" Why hadn't she asked me or anyone else to go with her?

"Alone means people won't disappoint me." She leveled me with a glare. "How could you?"

"I'm sorry." I stood again but she took another step away. "I'm so, so sorry. It was a mistake."

"You stole my chance to see her."

"I didn't know you'd want to."

Her stare narrowed. "That doesn't make it right."

"I know." I held up my hands. "Tell me what I can do. Please."

Kat didn't answer. Instead, she flew past me, going to the dresser and opening the top drawer. She scooped out the clothes she'd put in there when we'd arrived and rushed to the bed, flipping open her suitcase and dropping them inside. Then she did the same with the second drawer.

"Kat."

She shook her head, disappearing into the bathroom. The clink of plastic bottles being shoved into a bag echoed in the room.

"Kat, please," I said when she came back into the room, dropping her toiletry case into her purse. "I'm sorry. I didn't know. You never told me."

"Don't you dare blame this on me."

"I'm not." I held up my hands. "I'm only trying to

explain. I didn't know. You never talked about it. I made an assumption and it was the wrong one."

"Why would I talk about it?" She whirled on me, her face flushed and her eyes blazing. "Why would I talk about how my mother hated me? Why would I talk about living in the dirt for two years because sleeping in a trash heap, in a makeshift hovel with tarps and metal sheets and *mice*, was better than the alternative?"

"I'm—"

"Sorry?" She went to the suitcase, slamming it closed and zipping it tight. Then she turned to me, her hands planted on her hips. "I can't talk about that time. I don't want to relive those memories. Sure, we all pretend that living in the junkyard was this magical fairy tale. But it was scary. We were *scared*. You have no idea what it's like shivering yourself to sleep on cold nights and wishing you had just one more blanket. You don't know how it feels to wake up so hungry you can't see straight because all you had to eat the day before was half a peanut butter and honey sandwich on stale bread."

I struggled to breathe. The raw, ruthless emotion on her face cracked my heart.

"We were sixteen," she said. "So young and so foolish. But that was what life had dealt us and we made the best of it. Yes, there were some happy times. Yes, we were relatively safe. But the fear. You don't know what it's like to live in that kind of fear, so forgive me if I don't want to remember just so you and your family can talk about it over coffee."

She hefted her suitcase from the mattress and took three steps toward the door but stopped and turned again. "The reason I painted back then was because I needed something pretty. I needed to wake up to a world where I was in control. Where the flowers were pink and the sunshine was yellow because I said it was that way. It was the only control I had."

My throat was burning, but I managed a nod and a hoarse, "Okay."

"I stopped painting because I didn't need it. I wasn't scared anymore. When I came to Montana, I could wake up, look out the window and there was my magical meadow. There. In real life. For me to touch and know that tomorrow would be okay. I was safe because I'd found a home. And I was safe because I had you."

"You'll always have me."

She shook her head, blinking away a sheen of tears. "No, I won't."

"Kat, please." I closed the distance between us, putting my hands on her shoulders. "Don't go. Let's work this out."

"I'm such a fool." Her eyes filled with tears. "Pining after you for all these years. Hoping and dreaming that one day you'd love me the way I love you."

My heart dropped. She loved me? The words unknotted the twisting fear in my belly. If she loved me, then we'd figure this out. We'd be together and we'd find a way to put this behind us. We could overcome this, right?

I opened my mouth to tell her I was in love with her, to drop to my knees and plead with her to stay. But before I could, she stepped out of my hold and my hands sank like bricks in water to my sides.

"Thank you." Her voice was as icy as her glare. "You know what this trip was about? It was my chance to let you go, to stop wasting years waiting for you to love me. When you came along, I didn't think it would help. But here we are and now I have what I wanted. You're nothing to me now. Not even my friend."

"We're more than friends."

She turned and opened the door, her parting words ringing loud and clear even after the door slammed shut. "Not anymore."

CHAPTER FOURTEEN

CASH

In less than one week, I'd fallen in love with my best friend.

And in a single hour, I'd lost her.

I drummed my fingers on the reception desk, willing the man who'd disappeared behind the employees-only door to hurry the fuck up. My duffel bag rested at my feet. I'd tossed the clothes inside as haphazardly as Kat had done her own.

Stupid bastard that I was, her confession about loving me had sent me into a tailspin. When I should have been running after her, I'd stood frozen in the middle of our room.

It had probably only been five minutes, ten max, that I'd stood like a dumbfounded chump, but it had given her enough lead time to escape.

She loved me.

How long? How long had I been blind to the truth?

I'd realized, standing in that hotel room, there was a reason I constantly bought Kat trinkets and gifts and chocolate bars. When I saw something that would bring a smile to her face, I had to have it.

Just because.

Just because.

Just. Because.

Just because I was in love with her.

After shaking off my epiphany, I'd flown into action, packing while leaving a panicked message on her voicemail. Since then, I'd left six more and ten texts, none of which had been returned.

Damn, I was a fucking idiot, though idiot wasn't strong enough a word. Once I got Kat back—and I was getting her back—she could call me every awful thing from prick to asshole to douchebag that popped into that gorgeous head of hers and I'd agree with them all.

If she wanted to take a job in Oregon, then Heron Beach would be our home. I'd give up the ranch, the horses and that life, because she was worth it.

My mother had always told me the reason our ranch worked was because every generation had tackled it as a team. Granddad and Grandma. Mom and Dad. Easton and Gemma. They worked it together because that was what made it special. A partnership. Two halves making a whole.

And at the moment, my other half was nowhere to be found.

This time, I wasn't going to find Kat in the café or on the beach. She'd packed her bag and was either at another hotel, far away from me, or she'd hauled the Cadillac out of valet and was on her way to . . . anywhere. So I'd checked out of the room, then asked this clerk to find out if the Cadillac was still parked.

Had he gone to the parking lot or garage or wherever the hell they kept the cars to check himself? How hard was it to find out if a ticket had been claimed for a goddamn car?

Beside me, a couple laughed as they checked into their room. They couldn't keep their hands off each other. *Honeymooners.* They'd been telling anyone who'd listen.

That should be me and Kat. We should be the ones kissing and smiling and anxious to get behind a closed door to strip our clothes off.

I dragged a hand through my hair. *Come on. Come on.* What was taking so long?

My eyes were glued to the door where he'd disappeared. My foot tapped on the floor. If they'd just tell me where they parked the cars, I'd go find out if the Cadillac was there myself.

I dug my phone from my pocket and checked again for a message from Kat. *Nothing.* Where was she? Maybe this clerk would give me Aria's number. Had Kat told her where she was going? Were they together?

The door opened and I held my breath, but instead of the clerk, fucking Mark Gallaway emerged, wearing the same suit and smug grin he had in the café. Didn't that guy have a corner office to lurk in?

"Mr. Greer." He came around the desk, hand extended.

I shook it with a tad too much force. "Mr. Gallaway."

"Have you been helped?"

"Yes." *By your impossibly slow staff.* I should have been out the door ten minutes ago.

"Excellent. Enjoy your stay." He turned and took three steps away, his polished shoes clicking on the floor.

I wanted to watch that guy disappear and never see him again. I wanted to say fuck Mark Gallaway, I didn't need him to help me find Aria. But my pride was in tatters. It had been ripped to shreds by the five-foot-one woman who owned my heart. And above all else, I wanted her back.

"Wait," I called to Mark's back.

He turned and raised an eyebrow. "Yes?"

That son of a bitch knew where she was, didn't he? "I'm looking for Kat. Have you seen her?"

"I have."

I gritted my teeth. "And where was that?"

His smirk stretched as he sauntered my way, arrogance rolling over his shoulders. Swear to God, if she'd taken a job in the last hour while I'd been packing and searching for her, I'd . . .

Deal. I'd deal with it.

We'd do whatever she needed to do, even if that meant working for a man like Gallaway.

"I believe she left with Aria. Something about a road trip."

Fuck my life. "Thanks." The word tasted bitter. "If I asked, would you give me Aria's number?"

"Are you asking?"

"Yes." *Don't punch him. Don't punch him.*

He stared at me, cold and calculating. I expected the asshole to turn and walk away without another word, but I stood tall, patient, because he wasn't the only powerful man in the room. Maybe I didn't show it. I didn't need to wear an Italian suit or four-thousand-dollar watch.

But I wasn't backing down.

Kat was mine.

He could try to steal her and he'd lose.

She'd been mine for a long time, even when I hadn't wanted to admit it to myself.

Kat had said something on the trip, during our first fight. *Why do you let people decide how your life is going to go?* God, she'd pissed me off.

She was wrong about people pushing me into a certain job. I'd always gone willingly. Except maybe that statement wasn't entirely wrong, she'd just pegged the wrong target.

My family's influence over my relationship with Kat

was stronger than I'd let myself recognize. They'd dictated that she be a family member. I'd followed their lead.

But Kat wasn't only my friend. She wasn't only my best friend.

She was mine.

She'd been mine since the day a young stallion had bucked me off into a fence and I'd gotten a concussion. She'd crept into my room every two hours that night, waking me as the doctor had instructed to make sure I was okay.

She'd been mine since the night she'd gotten so drunk at a bonfire party that she'd decided my bed was more comfortable than hers and had crawled in next to me, snoring so loud I'd heard it down the hallway from the living room where I'd slept on the couch.

She'd been mine since day one.

And whether Mark Gallaway gave me Aria's phone number or not, I'd find her. I'd search every highway in the country until I tracked her down.

Mark's eyes narrowed as I held his gaze. I stood steady and strong until, finally, he reached inside his jacket and pulled out a phone, scrolling through before rattling off Aria's number.

"Did you need me to write it down?" he asked.

"No." I mentally repeated it once. Twice. Then it was there. "Appreciated."

He gave me a nod, then turned again. I didn't wait for him to disappear. I went back to my spot at the desk, took out my phone and let my fingers fly across the screen as I called Aria's number.

It rang three times before it clicked to voicemail. "Aria, this is Cash Greer. I'm looking for Kat. Please have her call me."

I ended that call and dialed Kat's again. It went straight to voicemail. "Kat. Please. Let's talk about this. Please call me back." I sent the same in a text, sending it off just as the clerk returned.

"I'm sorry for the delay, sir."

"That's fine," I lied.

"It looks like that car is no longer in valet."

Son of a bitch. Where had she gone? She couldn't have gotten far, but I was without wheels and unsure of the direction to head.

"Is there anything else I can assist you with?" the clerk asked.

"No, thanks." I bent and picked up my bag, only to turn back again. "Is there a rental car place in town?"

"Yes." He took a sheet of paper from beneath the counter—a map. Staring at it upside down, he circled the destination and used a highlighter to mark directions from the hotel.

"Thanks again." I took the map and wasted no time walking the five blocks to the rental place.

It took another thirty minutes to rent a car. People in Heron Beach didn't seem to be in much of a hurry. The nervous energy I was emitting didn't inspire them to work with much urgency either. Finally, with the keys to a black SUV in my hand, I loaded up my bag and got behind the wheel.

But where was I going?

Kat and Aria hadn't returned a call or text, so I made a different call instead, bracing because I knew it was going to sting. I sucked in a deep breath as the phone rang and when my mother's voice answered, I blew it out in a shaky stream.

"Hello! I was wondering when you'd call."

"Hey, Mom."

"Uh-oh. What's wrong?"

There was no hiding anything from Liddy Greer. At least, not if you were her son. "I fucked up, Mom. I need your help."

"I'm listening."

I spewed the story in a rambled rush. Mom stayed quiet on the line as I spoke, and replaying the story, hearing my own words again, was nearly as bad as having to confess it to Kat.

"Cash." She was shaking her head at me. I didn't need to see it to know. "You fucked up."

"I know." It wasn't often that Mom said fuck, or any variation. For her to curse, I hadn't just fucked up, I'd done it royally. "I can't find her. She's not answering my calls, and I can't lose her like this."

"Maybe you should."

I flinched. "What?"

"Maybe you need to let her go. I know she's your friend and you care about her. But son—"

"I'm in love with her."

My declaration was met with a deafening hush. Wouldn't Mom want us together? Maybe I didn't deserve Kat, especially after all I'd done to hurt her, but damn it, I'd spend the rest of my life righting my years of wrongs.

"Mom," I whispered. "Please."

"You're sure you love her?"

"Took me a while to figure it out but she's the one."

Mom sniffled.

"What? Why is that wrong?"

"Oh, it's not wrong. It's just about damn time." She laughed. "What can I do?"

I sighed. "She won't take my calls and I don't know where she's at."

"Okay. Let me see what I can do," Mom said, then ended the call.

Waiting and sitting idle was not an option, so I started the rental car and pulled up my GPS app.

Kat couldn't have gone far, but if she was racing down the highway, a ten- or twenty-minute lead meant it would take me hours to catch up. That was, if I even started in the right direction. At least one thing in my favor was Kat's propensity to always drive the speed limit.

Had she started home? Kat could be miles on her way to Montana. Maybe she'd changed her mind about California after all, though I doubted it. She could have taken that quarter and let it decide.

They were all options, but I didn't punch Clear River or Temecula into the navigation. My gut said Kat was with Aria.

So I was headed toward Welcome, Arizona.

CHAPTER FIFTEEN

KATHERINE

"Damn, girl," Aria said. "I'm sorry."

"I hate him," I lied, my fingers tightening around the wheel. We both knew I'd never hate Cash.

Over the past thirty minutes, I'd told Aria everything that had happened today. Everything I hadn't when I'd found her at the hotel with my suitcase in hand to say goodbye.

Aria had known something was wrong, but rather than push me to talk or let me leave, she'd stuck close. Loyalty was my second favorite quality of hers, the first being her ability to listen. As the Cadillac flew down the highway, she sat in the passenger seat, attuned to my every word.

We were on the highway that would eventually lead us to Arizona. Maybe after twelve hundred miles I wouldn't feel quite so broken.

I'd set out on this trip to get over Cash. To put the

hopes and dreams of an *us* in my rearview mirror. Maybe one day I'd stop loving him, but what hurt the worst was that I'd lost my friend.

My best friend.

He was the one I ran to on bad days. He was my safe haven. When I'd gotten food poisoning from grocery store sushi, he'd been the one holding my hair back as I puked for twelve hours. When one of our guests had sent me a scathing email about his bad experience with allergies at the resort—as if I had some control over the pollen in the air—Cash had let me cry on his shoulder and mourn the loss of my impeccable five-star Google rating.

His absence was like a gaping hole in my heart.

But at least I had Aria.

After I'd left Cash standing in the room, the truth tainting the air, I'd hurried to the front desk to page Aria. She'd come into the lobby with a smile that had brought me to tears. I'd hugged her, told her I was leaving and that I was so happy to have found her again. I'd apologized for the last-minute change of plan but I wasn't leaving her with the Cadillac.

I needed it to make my escape.

Without asking why I was seconds away from an emotional breakdown, she'd grabbed my free hand and hauled me to the second floor, winding through a maze of hallways until we reached Mark's office. I'd waited in the hallway while she'd gone inside to talk to him. When she'd come out, she'd looked at me and said, "Let's go."

On the way out of town, we'd stopped by her home so she could pack a bag and ask her neighbor to water her plants.

She seemed used to taking time off. To stepping away. Maybe this trip of mine wouldn't have been such a disaster if I'd taken more vacations before this. Maybe I would have realized much sooner that I was replaceable at work and that the family I'd clung to wouldn't bother to call for days, not even Gemma.

The open road ahead did nothing to give me a sense of freedom. Instead I looked down the double yellow lines that divided the pavement and felt lost. Alone. Where was I going? Arizona was a start, but then where? What was I doing with my life?

I just wanted . . . I wanted to go home. I wanted to rewind this week and go back to the days when I wasn't so angry at Cash I could barely breathe.

"You okay?" Aria asked.

"No."

"Want me to drive?"

I clutched the wheel. Having it under my palms felt like the only thing in my control at the moment. "No, thanks."

Her phone rang in her hand and she narrowed her eyes at the number. "Um . . ."

"What?"

"Area code four-oh-six."

"It's Cash."

"Should I answer it?"

"Definitely not." He'd been calling me relentlessly and sending texts. My phone rested on the seat, tucked beneath my knee. I'd felt it vibrating and held tighter to the wheel every time, resisting any temptation to answer.

"He really didn't say anything when you said you loved him?" Aria asked.

"Nothing." To be fair, I hadn't really given him the chance.

He'd looked so shocked, like a deer in the headlights. Of all the things he'd said to me in that hotel room, his silence had by far hurt the worse.

"I hate him," I whispered. *I love him.* Even furious, my heart belonged to him.

"I'm sorry about your mom," Aria said.

"Me too."

I'd been wrestling with feelings for my mother for years. I was sorry that she'd died. I was sorry that she'd lived a life without much joy. But I didn't forgive her and I doubted I ever would. She'd hurt me too deeply, and even if I'd had the chance to see her again, even if she'd apologized, I wouldn't have wanted a relationship with her.

Did I blame Cash for her death? No. She'd given me up long, long ago. A visit to Montana wasn't enough to compensate for her actions. And I knew, bone deep, that Cash had only done what he'd thought was best.

Bone deep, I'd already forgiven him for always looking out *for my own good.*

My phone rang again, vibrating against my jeans. Temptation got the better of me and I slid it free, surprised to see Liddy's name on the screen.

"Who is it?" Aria asked.

"Cash's mom."

It rang in my hand as I alternated my gaze from the phone to the road.

"Are you going to answer?"

"He probably called her." That or she was finally returning my call. Any other person, I would have ignored it. But this was Liddy, the woman I loved more than my own mother, so I answered. "Hi."

"We love you," she said.

I blinked. "Huh?"

"We love you," she repeated. "No matter what happens with you and Cash, we *all* love you. He wants me to find out where you are. He's desperate, Kat. But I'm going to hang up before you can even tell me. Do what you need to do for you. And we'll be here whenever you're ready to come home."

I opened my mouth to speak, but Liddy had already hung up.

Just like that, she'd made me a promise. She'd erased all of my fears. No matter where I lived, no matter where I worked, she loved me. They all did.

Even Cash, in his own way.

God, this hurt. The ache in my heart twisted so hard it stole my breath and a little sob escaped my lips.

"Oh, Katherine." Aria placed her hand on my shoulder.

"I'm okay." My eyes flooded and I swiped at them, catching the tears before they could fall.

I'm okay.

This was just another bump in the road. Another unexpected turn. I'd deal with it like all the bumps that had come before. On my own.

Aria and I drove in silence, the whirl of the tires offering no comfort. The scenery was lush and green, and though we were headed away from the ocean, its salt still clung to the air.

It was nice. Different. Except I didn't want different. I wanted to breathe in the clean Montana mountain air, smelling hay and horses as I watched Cash work.

Training the younger animals was his favorite. Cash would spend hours with a foal, teaching it in slow, methodical steps how to wear a halter and follow a lead. Then as the horses got older, he'd teach them to wear a saddle on their backs and a bit in their mouths.

It was magic, watching him work, and one of my favorite pastimes. He was the definition of steady. Gentle. Patient. I'd stand at the arena's fence, unable to tear my eyes away. Every few minutes, he'd glance my direction and gift me with a smile.

That smile.

There had always been love in Cash's smile.

Liddy had said he was desperate. Desperate for what? To find me and apologize again? Or was there more?

I'd run from him so fast today that I hadn't given him the chance to explain. I'd shut him out and thrown up my guard. I claimed to love him but hadn't truly let him in.

Tears filled my eyes again and no amount of biting my cheek would make them stop. They fell in silent streams down my cheeks, dripping onto my jeans and creating dark indigo circles as they fell.

My foot came off the gas. "I'm so sorry, Aria. I can't do this."

She gave me a sad smile. "I understand."

"I just . . . I can't run from this." From my home. From my family. *From him.*

"What about Cash?" she asked.

"I don't know." I sighed. "I'm mad."

"Uh, yeah." She nodded. "I would be too."

Though with every passing minute, my anger was subsiding. He shouldn't have kept my mother's visit a secret, but I understood why he had.

We all love you. Liddy's words rang in my ears. We *all* love you. What was she getting at?

"I can't exactly avoid him forever," I said. "We'll figure it out eventually. But there's no rush. A few more hours to let things settle won't hurt."

"I wouldn't count on that if I were you."

"Huh?"

She glanced over her shoulder and through the back window. "He's been behind us for the past few minutes."

"What?" My eyes whipped to the mirror, where a black SUV was nearly clinging to my bumper. I'd been so focused on the road ahead, I hadn't noticed it approach.

The SUV's headlights flashed and a strong, sinewy arm extended out the driver's side window, waving to get my attention.

My breath hitched. I knew that arm.

I let the Cadillac drift slower, my foot barely pressing the brake as I scanned the side of the road for a place to pull over. A mailbox caught my eye ahead, marking the entrance to a private driveway. I put on my blinker, slowing down as Cash eased back to give me some space so we could both pull off the highway.

"I'll just wait here." Aria grinned as I opened the door.

I stepped onto the ground, my feet barely steady, as Cash rushed to me, sweeping me into his arms in a crushing embrace.

My hands dug into his shoulders, holding tight. I wasn't sure if I was gripping him so strongly because I was trying to punish him or because he'd come after me. But I didn't protest as he held me tightly against his chest, lifting me off my feet until they dangled by his shins.

"I'm sorry." His voice was filled with pain and regret. "God, Kat. I'm sorry."

"I forgive you."

He pulled away and his eyebrows came together. "You do?"

"I'm hurt, but I forgive you. Your heart was in the right place." And in his boots, I might have done the same. I wouldn't have wanted him to be hurt by a woman who'd take my money without even asking about her child.

"Doesn't matter." He shook his head and set me down. "I should have told you."

My shoulders sagged and I nodded. "It's done."

What was the point of staying mad at him? It wouldn't change anything. It wouldn't undo the past and it wouldn't change the relationship I'd had with my mother.

I glanced past him to the SUV. "How'd you know where I was going?"

"Lucky guess."

I looked up and met those hazel eyes. "Why'd you come?"

"Because I love you."

My heart dropped. My mouth went dry. "What?"

Cash stepped closer, taking my face in his hands. "I love you, Katherine Gates."

This wasn't actually happening. How long had I dreamed of hearing those words? How long had I hoped for them? Too long. It was impossible to believe they were real. "As a friend."

He shook his head. "Not as a friend."

"As a little sister."

That earned me another head shake. "Definitely not as a little sister."

"You love me?"

"I am *in love* with you."

Cash was in love with me. My head spun as it tried to flip the switch from fantasy to reality. I opened my mouth to say something, anything, but there were no words.

Actually, there were three.

"I love you."

Cash's entire body radiated relief. He flashed me that sexy grin, giving me a split second to enjoy it, before he slammed his mouth down on mine. His kiss was so consuming, so powerful and adoring, it felt like he was claiming me forever, branding me as his and his alone.

He loved me.

The fears, doubts and insecurities I'd clutched for years were swept away with his hot tongue. The internal box that had guarded my secrets, and my heart, was wide open.

The blare of the Cadillac's horn filled the air. "Get a room!"

I giggled at Aria as Cash broke away, holding me tight.

"I love you, Kat," he whispered.

"I love you, Cash."

"Don't go," he pleaded. "Stay with me. Lean on me. I swear, I won't let you fall."

I dropped my head to his chest. The only man in the

world who could make me that promise, make me believe it, was Cash. "Okay."

The passenger door to the Cadillac popped open and Aria stepped out, rounding the trunk to join us. "Hi, Cash."

"Hi, Aria."

"How fast were you going to catch us?" she asked.

He grinned. "Fast enough."

A semitruck blazed down the highway, the noise so loud it reminded me that we were essentially on the side of the road. "Should we head back to the hotel?"

"I've got a better idea." Cash shook his head and walked past me to the Cadillac. He leaned inside and when he stood, he held up the quarter I'd left in the tray. The quarter Carol had given me. "How about we start this adventure over?"

Drive wherever the quarter intended. Explore the countryside with the man I loved. Share hotel rooms and sleep in each other's arms. "Yes, please."

"Would you take the Cadillac?" Cash asked Aria.

"Of course." She stepped closer and took me in one of her fierce hugs.

I clung to her, holding her close. "Thank you. For everything."

"Thanks for coming to find me." She let me go and leaned back. "I've missed you."

We didn't need to voice that we'd see one another

again. We didn't need to say call me or text. Now that I'd found Aria again, I wasn't going to lose her.

"Nice to meet you, Cash." She held out her hand.

He shook it, then pulled her in for a hug. "Don't be a stranger. Come see us in Montana."

"Will you teach me to ride a horse?"

He chuckled and let her go. "You got it."

"Will you be okay driving to Arizona alone?" I asked Aria as Cash went to collect my suitcase and belongings from the Cadillac.

"Of course, but not today. I'm going home. I have to work on Monday."

"What?" My mouth fell open. "But the trip—"

"Oh, I figured he'd catch up with us after about an hour or two." She winked at Cash as he slammed the trunk.

"How'd you know?"

"Please." She rolled her eyes. "That man loves you too much to let you go."

I cast a glance at Cash, where he was hauling my purse from the backseat. And I loved him too much to actually run away.

Aria and I shared one last hug, then she waved goodbye to Cash and climbed in the Cadillac, flipping it around and disappearing down the highway.

"Think we'll ever see that car again?" Cash asked, pulling me into his side.

"No."

That car had taken me on the trip that I'd needed, just like it had with Londyn and Gemma.

Cash led me to the passenger door of the SUV, closing it for me once I was inside. Then he jogged around the hood and slid behind the wheel, holding the quarter up between us.

I took it from his fingers and gave it a flip. "Heads left. Tails right."

———

"HEY," I answered Gemma's call.

Cash touched his invisible watch, reminding me that we were kind of in the middle of something, but I held up a finger. I wouldn't have answered except it was the first time on the trip that she'd called, and I wanted to make sure everything was okay with her and the baby.

"Hi," she whispered. "How are you?"

"Fine. Why are you whispering?"

"Because I'm breaking the rules by calling you and if Carol finds out, she's going to banish me from the lodge."

"What rules?"

"We're not allowed to interrupt your vacation. Carol's orders. She wanted you to have time to disconnect and explore and whatever. I would have broken the rule sooner but she promised to make me a fresh cherry pie and I was waiting until she delivered."

Carol. So she was the reason that my phone calls and

texts had gone unanswered. I should have expected her to lay down the law with the family like she had with the resort staff.

The only contact we'd had with home over the past four days was when Cash had called Liddy, assuring her that we were together and that everything had worked out. He'd also asked that she not tell anyone that the two of us were together before we had a chance to tell them ourselves when we got home.

"So where are you? How's it going? Did you and Cash hook up yet?"

"Did Liddy tell you?"

"What?" Her voice got louder. "You hooked up? And Liddy knows? Why didn't she tell me?"

"If she didn't tell you, how did you know?"

"It was only a matter of time. You two needed to get away and do something without everyone in the family watching over your shoulders so he could realize how wonderful and beautiful you are and the idiot would finally pull his head out of his ass and fall in love with you."

"Thanks, Gem," Cash muttered at my side.

I laughed. "You're on speaker."

"Oh," she muttered. "Well, I stand by my statement. Hi, Cash."

"Hi," he said. "When you made me camp out and search for a mountain lion, there wasn't really a lion, was there?"

"Nope."

And his appearance the morning I'd been slated to leave hadn't been coincidence either. It was why she'd made me take cookies. Why she'd had Easton go fill the car with gas.

I'd hug Gemma for that later and bake her a dozen cherry pies.

"Where are you?" she asked. "When are you coming home? I'm bored. So, so bored. Carol took this activity rest restriction from the doctor to the extreme. She has me at the front desk and I'm slowly losing my mind. And you should know that things are totally falling apart around here."

"Really?" A smile spread across my face. "That's great!"

"It is?" Cash asked and I waved him off.

"What's happening?" I asked Gemma.

"Well, let's see. Annabeth got into a huge fight with one of the housekeepers and the two of them made this big scene in front of a guest. It was wildly uncomfortable and Easton had to step in. You can imagine how well he handled that."

I cringed. "Who'd he fire?"

"Both of them. But Carol rehired them ten minutes later."

"Okay." That was going to take some fixing. It had to have been bad because Annabeth wasn't one to lose her composure. My guess was the stress of my absence was taking its toll. My chest swelled with pride.

I'd feel guilty about that later, but at the moment, I was just happy that they hadn't been perfect without me.

"That's not all," Gemma said. "Chef Wong has gone rogue."

I scrunched up my nose. "He does that at times." Hence the warning I'd given Carol.

"When JR walked into the kitchen and found him making tofu instead of beef, things got dicey."

Cash chuckled, glancing over to the woman at the counter.

She nodded and said, "We're ready for you, sir."

"I'll call and check in with Annabeth tomorrow," I told Gemma. "And I'll call Chef Wong."

"Good. We need you. So when are—"

"Hey, who are you talking to?" Carol's voice carried through the phone.

"Oh, shit," Gemma hissed, then called out, "No one!" The line was silent for a long moment until she returned. "Phew. That was close."

Cash jerked his chin and reached for the red circle to end the call but I swatted him away.

"Gemma, I have to let you go."

"When are you coming home?"

"We, um . . . we'll probably need another week."

"Ten days," Cash corrected just as the wedding march rang over the speaker system. There was a large diamond ring on my finger, one Cash had given me last night on bended knee.

"Wait, what is that?" Gemma asked. "Katherine Gates, are you elop—"

Cash ended the call, took the phone from my hand and tucked it into his jeans pocket, where he'd kept our quarter. He'd taken ownership of flipping the coin over the past four days and fate—as he'd called it, though we both knew it wasn't coincidence—had brought us to Las Vegas. To the Clover Chapel.

He led me toward the aisle. "I love you, Mrs. Greer."

"I'm not Mrs. Greer yet."

"Close enough." My soon-to-be husband framed my face with his hands and dropped a kiss to my lips.

The same soft kiss he gave me after Elvis pronounced us husband and wife.

EPILOGUE

KATHERINE

F*ive months later . . .*
"Don't touch my hair," I whispered.

Cash's hands, centimeters from a curl I'd spent two minutes perfecting, stopped beside my ears. He brought them forward, toward my cheeks.

"Don't touch my face."

He grumbled and shot me a scowl. He was midstroke, his cock buried deep inside my throbbing core. "Then where can I touch?"

"Anywhere below the waist."

Cash pulled out, grabbed me by the hips, yanking me away from the counter, and spun me around before sinking deep.

I moaned, letting my head sag to the side.

Cash's hands dug into the flesh of my hips. His lips

found the sensitive skin below my ear, and even though it was dangerously close to the makeup I'd spent an hour on, the nip of his teeth was too good to pass up. "Fuck, but you feel good."

I hummed, rocking back against him as he thrust in and out.

His hand slipped beneath my shirt, his rough fingers sliding over my belly, dipping lower until his middle finger found my clit. He strummed the hard nub, bringing me closer and closer. My legs trembled, my heart raced. I was so close, I gasped, ready to detonate—

"Kat?" Jake's voice came from the hallway as he knocked on the door. "Are you in there?"

Cash froze.

My gaze whipped to the doorknob. *Locked.* I blew out a breath. "Y-yeah?"

"She's in the bathroom, Carol!" he yelled down the hallway.

"Tell her the photographer's here."

"Honey, the photographer's here," Jake repeated.

Cash began moving again, his finger swirling.

I caught his gaze in the mirror and the bastard was grinning. "Glad you find this so funny," I hissed.

He wouldn't be laughing if we got caught screwing in his grandparents' guest bathroom.

"Kat?" Jake called again. "Did you hear me?"

"I-I'm"—*oh my God*—"coming."

White spots broke across my vision and I exploded, feeling nothing but pulse after pulse of blinding pleasure as Cash continued his delicious torment.

Cash groaned, dropping his face to my shoulder right before he let go, his orgasm hard and fast like my own.

When we'd both regained our breath, I lifted my heavy lids and smiled at our reflection. "I love you."

"I love you too, sweetheart." He wrapped his arms around me, holding me tight for a long moment before sliding out and tucking himself into his jeans. Then he bent and pulled my panties up my legs and smoothed down the skirt of my dress.

The whole family was at Carol and Jake's place for Friday night dinner. Except we'd had to arrive two hours early because before our regular weekly meal, we were having photos taken before sunset. The whole crew was going to hike out behind the house to a grove of cotton-wood trees brimming with gold and orange leaves. In all my years in Montana, I'd never seen a prettier fall.

The photos were for the resort website—my idea. It was time to update the family photo with all of the Greers, including the cutest addition, Gemma and Easton's two-and-a-half-month-old baby boy.

I straightened the sleeves on my green dress and looked down at the skirt to make sure there weren't any wrinkles. My knee-high boots were polished and I did a quick fluff of my hair.

Cash tucked in his starched white shirt and rebuckled his belt. Later tonight, I was stripping him down to nothing and having my way with him again. This bathroom escapade had only been a preview of later.

We had a lot to celebrate.

This morning, the two of us had spent another few minutes in a bathroom—the one we shared at home—as we'd waited for the results of three pregnancy tests.

Next year, we'd have to retake photos with our own baby Greer. I doubted anyone would mind.

"Should we tell them?" I asked as Cash leaned into the mirror to wipe the hint of gloss I'd left behind.

"Do you want to tell them?"

He looked down at me and grinned. "Yeah."

"Good. Me too."

I wasn't waiting months to tell our family we were having a baby. Besides, as soon as Carol realized I wasn't drinking the bottle of wine she'd brought for me tonight, the secret would be out.

Our family hadn't been thrilled about the fact that we'd eloped and excluded them from a momentous occasion, but they'd all been so happy to see Cash and me together, their irritation hadn't lasted long. Plus we'd thrown a huge reception so they'd at least gotten a party.

Besides Friday night dinners, that had been our only night out since returning home. Not only had Cash and I been savoring our extra time alone, merging bedrooms and closets, but he'd been consumed with work.

The training facility was up and running and for the past month, Cash had worked tirelessly to train his own staff as well as the new animals. Easton's lack of communication with his brother had rubbed me the wrong way, but Cash had confronted him about it when we'd gotten home. Easton had apologized and ever since, there had been no question about who ran the equine center. No decisions were made by anyone but Cash.

I was proud of him for how hard he'd been working. He'd already been interviewed by a major horse magazine, and breeders from all over the Pacific Northwest were clamoring for him to see their horses.

He was as happy as I'd ever seen him. Energized and excited. We both were. But work wasn't the best part of my day anymore. Coming home to Cash, sharing this life with him, was my dream come true.

"Okay." I smoothed my dress down once more. "You go out first."

Cash lifted my hand to his lips, kissing my knuckles, then gave me the sexy smirk that had brought us to the bathroom in the first place. He eased out the door and I counted to ten, hoping not to draw any notice when I joined my husband and the others downstairs.

Gemma was sitting on the couch, nursing the baby, when I reached the living room. "Your cheeks are a little flushed, Katherine. You weren't doing something naughty in the bathroom, were you?"

"Shut up." I sat beside her. "It's not like you and Easton haven't done the same thing."

"Touché." She peeked beneath her cover-up at the baby, her eyes softening at her son. "Your phone was buzzing while you were . . . indisposed."

I reached for my purse on the end table beside the couch where I'd left it when we'd come inside and pulled out my phone. "It was Aria."

"Call her back," Gemma said. "We have time and I'd like to say hi."

Aria answered on the first ring. "Hey!"

"Hey. You're on speaker. I'm here with Gemma."

"Hi, mama. What are you guys doing?"

Gemma smiled. "We're getting ready for family pictures."

"I've never done those before," Aria said.

"Me neither," Gemma said.

"What are you doing?" I asked, hearing what sounded like wind in the background.

"I'm on my way to Arizona." She whooped. "Finally. Though I'm tempted to keep this car forever and not tell Londyn. It's been so much fun to drive all summer."

Aria hadn't been able to get away from work for a while, but we'd all assured her there was no rush. One of her staff members had quit and with the busy tourist season, she'd needed to stay close to The Gallaway. Clara and her son, August, had visited Oregon and offered to drive it to California, but Aria had insisted on driving it to Arizona. She was committed to this handoff.

"Drive safely," I said.

"I will. I have two weeks off and I'm in no rush. Clara's asshole of a boss is going to be gone when I get there so that's a bonus."

Gemma and I shared a look.

Aria and I had talked often since my trip to Oregon. She'd also reconnected with Gemma and Londyn, bringing Clara into the loop too. The five of us had a weekly girls' night video chat. It had originally started as a book club but after six chats where no one had mentioned a book, we'd called it what it was—wine club. Though I'd be switching to sparkling grape juice for the next nine months.

Clara hadn't been able to make last week's chat. Her boss had needed some last-minute help preparing for a trip to Europe. But Aria had been there and she'd spent the first ten minutes of the call reminding us that Clara's boss —Broderick "Brody" Carmichael—was a prick. She'd even done the air quotes around his nickname.

Gemma and I suspected that Aria's hate maybe wasn't hate at all.

It was too bad Brody was going to be gone while she visited Arizona. Two weeks with the billionaire might have made for an interesting wine club chat.

"Text me when you get there," I said. "And say hi to Clara."

"Will do. Bye."

"She's got a thing for the boss," Gemma said, carefully detaching the baby as I put my phone away.

"Totally." I draped a cloth over my shoulder and reached for baby Jake. "I'll burp him so you can freshen up."

"Thanks," she said and handed him over before disappearing into the powder room.

I kissed Jake's cheek as I patted his back. His hair was thick and dark like Easton's. I suspected our baby would have the same.

"You're going to be a cousin," I whispered. "Do you think we'll have a girl or a boy?"

He answered with a juicy belch.

"Yeah, I'm thinking boy too."

Gemma returned, looking beautiful in her sage dress, and the two of us walked outside, me carrying the baby, to where everyone else was standing around the photographer on the front lawn.

Easton came over and took his son from my arms. "Hey, bud. Did you get a snack?"

The baby burped again, causing his father to chuckle.

"Okay." Carol clapped, her smile wide. "Everybody ready?"

After a chorus of nods, Jake took her hand and the two of them led the family around the corner of the house.

JR held out his elbow to escort Liddy behind his parents.

Easton tucked the baby in the crook of an arm and laced his fingers with Gemma's before the three of them set out across the lawn with the photographer.

Leaving me and Cash to trail behind.

I took one step onto the grass but he put his hand on my elbow to stop me.

"I have something for you." He reached into his pocket, pulling out a square, velvet box.

"What is this?"

He handed it to me. "Open it."

I lifted the lid, revealing a diamond bracelet, and gasped. "Cash, it's beautiful."

"There was a guest here a few years ago," he said, taking the jewelry from the box and clasping it around my wrist. "Some famous author you loved. She had a bracelet like this and you told me twice how much you loved the style. Simple and elegant—something like that."

Not something. Those had been my exact words and he'd remembered. How long had that been? Seven years? Eight?

Part of me wished we had figured it out sooner. That we'd realized there had always been more than friendship between us. And the other part of me was happy exactly the way our love story had played out. Because looking back on those moments of friendship, knowing that Cash knew me better than any person dead or alive, made these little moments precious.

I rolled my wrist, letting the diamonds catch the light,

then looked into my husband's sparkling hazel eyes. They were prettier than diamonds and I hoped our baby would inherit them.

"What is this for?"

He brushed a kiss to my lips, then took my hand, leading us on the path to our family. "Just because."

———

THE RUNAWAY SERIES continues with Forsaken Trail.

FORSAKEN TRAIL

Aria Saint-James has planned the perfect getaway: sweatpants, takeout and two weeks alone with her sister and nephew. Nowhere on that list is wearing a low-cut dress and uncomfortable heels to attend a wedding where she knows neither the bride nor the groom. Toss in her nemesis, Brody Carmichael, and her road trip to Arizona is officially a bust.

But at least there is champagne.

She blames the bubbly for falling into bed with Brody that night. Enemy or no, the billionaire is irresistible in a tux. But after their one-night tryst, Aria has no choice but to cut her vacation short, returning home to escape his devilish smile, vowing never to see Brody again.

Except Aria gets a surprise a few weeks later—she's pregnant. When he learns that she's carrying his child,

Brody offers Aria the chance of a lifetime. The catch? She has to live under his roof until the baby is born.

Either they'll kill each other in nine months. Or discover love buried beneath their hate.

ACKNOWLEDGMENTS

Thank you for reading *Quarter Miles*! I'm so thankful you picked up a copy of Katherine and Cash's story.

Special thanks to my editing and proofreading team: Elizabeth Nover, Julie Deaton, Karen Lawson and Judy Zweifel. Thank you to Sarah Hansen for the cover. Thanks to my agent, Kimberly Brower.

A huge thanks to Perry Street. I couldn't have asked for a better group of readers to follow me along on this journey. Your support and excitement truly mean the world to me. Thank you to the incredible bloggers who read and help me with promoting new books. I am beyond grateful for all the work you do to support me and the romance community. To the Goldbrickers, thanks for motivating me to 2000 every single day.

And lastly, to my friends and family. You are the fuel that keeps me going. Thank you!

ABOUT THE AUTHOR

Devney is a *USA Today* bestselling author who lives in Washington with her husband and two sons. Born and raised in Montana, she loves writing books set in her treasured home state. After working in the technology industry for nearly a decade, she abandoned conference calls and project schedules to enjoy a slower pace at home with her family. Writing one book, let alone many, was not something she ever expected to do. But now that she's discovered her true passion for writing romance, she has no plans to ever stop.

Don't miss out on Devney's latest book news.
Subscribe to her newsletter!
www.devneyperry.com

Made in the USA
Columbia, SC
04 March 2024

32675425R00155

Quarter Miles

USA TODAY BESTSELLING AUTHOR

DEVNEY PERRY

Editing & Proofreading:

Elizabeth Nover, Razor Sharp Editing

www.razorsharpediting.com

Julie Deaton, Deaton Author Services

www.facebook.com/jdproofs

Karen Lawson, The Proof is in the Reading

Judy Zweifel, Judy's Proofreading

www.judysproofreading.com

Cover:

Sarah Hansen © Okay Creations

www.okaycreations.com